Rita

My Lady Coquette

Vol. III

Rita

My Lady Coquette
Vol. III

ISBN/EAN: 9783337053413

Printed in Europe, USA, Canada, Australia, Japan

Cover: Foto ©Andreas Hilbeck / pixelio.de

More available books at **www.hansebooks.com**

BY

"RITA,"

AUTHOR OF "VIVIENNE," "LIKE DIAN'S KISS,"
"COUNTESS DAPHNE," ETC.

IN THREE VOLUMES.

VOL. III.

TINSLEY BROTHERS,
CATHERINE STREET, STRAND,
LONDON.
1881.

MY LADY COQUETTE.

CHAPTER I.

IR EDWARD LLEWELLYN gets very little satisfaction from his visit to the editor of the *Ystrad-ffeller Express.* He is a cringing low-born tradesman, who by dint of struggling and some poor pretence of learning, has won himself this position. From his account it appears that the notice had been forwarded to the publishing office, written in a clear, bold hand, and bearing the seal and motto of the Lle-wellyns on paper and envelope. When Sir

Edward sees the document, he recognises his own usual writing-paper easily enough ; but still he is at a loss to imagine what member of his household could have had the audacity to play such a practical joke.

He knows nothing of such a sheet of paper and envelope given to Rose Bertram on the day of her arrival at the Hall by Miss Llewellyn, and sent by Rose to Jane Croft at Llwynpia House in compliance with that young lady's urgent request for the crest of the Llewellyns.   Even if he had known of such a circumstance, his honest, not over-quick intellect, would have seen no connecting link between the two facts, for how could Jane Croft possibly interest herself in his affairs or those of Yolande Mervyn ?

After a sharp reprimand to the editor to be more careful on what authority he prints such paragraphs for the future, and a hint from that worthy man to the effect that, if people would only read their letters when they were received, it might save much after-confusion, the young baronet leaves the office and rides back gloomily to the Hall.

The report will, of course, be contradicted in the next week's issue of the paper ; but meanwhile hundreds may have seen and read it ; and there is no knowing how much mischief might have been done. His day's troubles are not half over, however ; for, on reaching home, he hears that Mrs Davies is waiting in the library to see him, and, on going thither, finds that worthy lady in a most distressed state of mind.

" Have you seen this ? " she cries, handing him a newspaper and utterly forgetting any other sort of greeting, so troubled and be-wildered does she feel.

" The *Express ?* " he says, in fierce annoyance at its haunting persistence. " Oh, yes ! I've just been to blow up the editor about it. I can't imagine who's done this."

" The *Express ?* No," returns Mrs Davies —" the *Times*—yesterday's *Times*."

"Good Heaven! it's not in that, surely?" cries the perplexed baronet, as he takes the proffered journal from her hand.

"Look there, in the list of marriages!" answers Mrs Davies. "Oh, dear, if Yolande sees it, it will kill her!"

Still with his own thoughts harping on that one subject about which he is concerned, Sir Edward looks stupidly at the list before him. The names are so numerous, the print is so small, and his own brain so confused, that he cannot for some moments distinguish anything bearing the importance Mrs Davies's words imply.

"There — there!" she says, impatiently, pointing to the place. "Don't you see, 'Charteris,' 'Ray'?"

He does see the words at last. With astonishment he reads the following announcement,—

"On the 5th inst., at Beechhampton Priory, Ashbourne, Devon, by special licence, Denzil Charteris, Esq. of Beechhampton, to

Pauline Ray, widow of the late Lauranston Ray, Esq."

He turns his eyes on Mrs Davies's pale troubled face, and the paper falls from his hand.

" It cannot be," he says aloud ; " there must be some mistake ! "

But, even as he says the words, he remembers the paragraph in the local paper, and the whole vile plot flashes across his mind. This is no mere hoax, no foolish joke ; it is part of a deep-laid scheme—a scheme to ruin the happiness of two people ; and he knows it has succeeded through his own fatal negligence. Had he but read the notice sent him, he would have inquired into the matter, and then it would have been stopped in time ; whereas now—now, alas, he cannot stay the mischief it has worked, he cannot avert the blow that will shatter the happiness of the girl he loves for ever !

" What is to be done ? " continues his companion, presently. " If Yolande were to hear of this in her weak and critical condition, it would kill her outright. Can you keep it from her ? "

" I must," he says, sternly. " I will give due warning to all those who come near her ; and you must keep back her letters for the present. As for my own course of action, I see it plainly now. I shall go to Beechhampton at once. Perhaps this is only a lie after all. I must see Charteris and explain."

" Then you might also go to Mervyn Court and tell the girls about Yolande's illness," suggests Mrs Davies, eagerly. " Say that we are doing everything necessary, and that the doctor says quiet and good nursing will soon bring her round. She has a good constitution fortunately. The only thing he fears is the winter coming on. Her chest will be so delicate after this. It is very likely she may have to go away to Italy or the south of France to set her up."

" Yes ; I will tell them," says Sir Edward,

with a heavy sigh. "I can but hope I may bring her back some good news, poor girl. How unfortunate that none of us thought of telling Charteris about her illness before!"

"It has all been so sudden and terrible you see," answers Mrs Davies. "After all, it is but a week too! Who could hav imagined so much happening in so short a time?"

Sir Edward is silent; his thoughts are busy with that other matter, of which Mrs Davies knows nothing as yet.

"Had Miss Mervyn any enemies here?" he asks, suddenly.

"Enemies?" cries the old lady, in surprise. "Certainly not—at least not that I am aware of. She was the idol of the whole school. They have been in despair since her illness."

"Well, at Ashbourne?" he continues, earnestly. "I ask for a special motive. It seems to me that some one has been maliciously tampering with her name and—and another person's, for reasons I cannot quite fathom yet. If you knew anything that would give me ever so faint a clue, it would be of great service at the present time. You see I cannot ask her."

Mrs Davies shakes her head gravely.

"No," she says, slowly, "I know no one who has such a feeling as you describe. But of course such a person may exist. I am not acquainted with her life at Mervyn Court, or any friends or enemies she may have made there."

"Ah, well, I must do my best to find out!" remarks Sir Edward. "And now, Mrs Davies, I will send my sister to you. You will need some refreshment before you return. I must go and prepare for my journey."

"Good-bye, and Heaven speed you!" she says, earnestly, as she takes his hand and looks up at his grave and troubled face. "I hope you may find things better than you imagine, and bring her lover back with you if possible. No one can breed dissension between them then."

He does not answer ; it sends a sharp thrill of pain to his heart to know that he has this task to perform, to seek the man who stands in the place he covets, and explain to him all the series of *contretemps* that one short week has wrought.

" Charteris was always so confoundedly jealous too," he thinks, as he turns away from the old lady's friendly face, and goes off to summon his valet and prepare for his hurried journey. " I hope, however, that he has not been such a fool as to marry another woman in such hot haste. Why, even if he received that paper, he might have waited longer than two days for confirmation of such a report ! Nothing would have induced me to believe ill of her, save from her own lips ! "

They were the very words Denzil Charteris had used in a love and trust as deep as that of the man who now thought them ; yet, tried by the same circumstances, perhaps he too might have been found wanting.

As fast as the express train can take him, does Sir Edward Llewellyn speed down to Devonshire, and at noon next day he drives over from Colston to Beechhampton.

" Yes ; Mr Charteris is at home," he is informed, rather doubtfully, the man going on to say that his master denies himself to all visitors ; " would Mrs Charteris do ? "

" Certainly not," answers Sir Edward, with terrible want of courtesy ; and he is just about to send in his card when a sudden thought flashes across him. If Charteris sees his name, it is not at all likely that he will be received ; so, after an instant's hesitation, he bids the man say he has called on important business.`

" Shall I say from Mr Herrick ? " asks Thompson, eagerly. " Mr Charteris receives no one but him."

" Yes, yes," answers Sir Edward, who does not know Mr Herrick, but looks upon the man's suggestion as a perfect godsend in this dilemma.

Accordingly he is shown into a small room fitted up like a study, and there left to await the master of the house. It may be five or ten minutes—Sir Edward does not know— when the opening of the door makes him turn round sharply.

" Good Heaven, Charteris, is it you ? " he says, and then his outstretched hand falls to his side.

Is this Charteris—this man gaunt and worn and white as ashes, with a fierce light burning in his deep dark eyes, the impress of a fearful misery on his haggard face ?

It is the look in those eyes that terrifies Sir Edward now, the look of madness, devil-wrought and murderous, that flashes over the face, till, with a quick-drawn breath and hand upraised to parry a frenzied blow, he gasps out,—

" Stay, Charteris ; it is a lie—all ! "

The haggard face before him changes, the

white lips part, yet no word comes. Sir Edward takes his arm and leads him to a chair as though he were a child.

"Listen," he says, in calm steady tones that insensibly control the ear of the miserable being who hears them. "She came to stay at the Park with my sister, and met with an accident while driving. She has been very ill, and could not write. Some blundering fool sent a gossiping notice to one of the local papers. Have you seen it?"

"Yes," he answers, hoarsely.

"Then it is as I suspected!" cries Sir Edward. "This is all part of a scheme to ruin her happiness and yours. One word more, Charteris. You did not believe it?"

"I did."

"But you are not lost to her? You did not distrust her quite so easily? You are not—"

"Married? Yes!"—and he laughs a laugh as mad and fierce as ever left a madman's lips in the solitude of his lonely cell.

Sir Edward shudders as he hears the sound.

"Then it is too late," he says, and sinks down into the opposite chair, with the misery of that other face reflected in his own. "How could you have doubted her so easily?" he groans aloud. "Could you not have waited, or written, or come, before putting this crowning barrier between her love and yours?"

"She does not love me!" exclaims the wretched man, wildly. "I have her own letter, in which she told me she was about to wed you. And when the paper came too, and I saw it printed there, I could doubt no longer."

"Oh, Heaven, what a net of misery you have woven!" cries Sir Edward, in despair. "The mistake, the letter, the doubts, all these could have been explained away; but nothing can undo the knot you have tied for yourself. Oh, Charteris, were you mad, to throw away your happiness thus?"

Denzil makes no answer. He only sits in stony, haggard misery, his senses coming slowly, uncertainly back, after the long and fearful strain of the past week. Piece by piece he puts together the framework of this puzzle ; drop by drop does his cup of wretchedness fill with every added proof. He has been duped and deceived by the woman whose only fault till now he deemed her too great love for him. Shudderingly he thinks of Yolande's parting words, "Don't mistrust me, whatever any one may say." And what has he done ? Not only believed ill of her, but in his madness bound himself to the woman who has worked this deadly wrong. Yes, he sees it all now so clearly—the cruel, horrible plot, the well-timed consolation and sympathy that soothed his anguish and whispered to the heart-wrung desolate man, " Am I not here, and do I not love you ten thousand times better than she ? Would I not rather have the dregs of your life and heart than the whole devotion and worship of another man ? "

He thinks of the love, the tenderness, the clinging beauty of the siren who bewitched him, who threw the glamour of the senses over his momentary madness, who worked upon his pride and outraged honour and falsified trust, who— But there he ceases.

A whirlwind of passion shakes him as a storm may shake a reed. He starts to his feet and throws his clasped hands wildly above him.

"O Heaven!" he cries, "shall I never cross this gulf that lies between my love and me? Shall I yearn for her unceasingly, knowing that my own mad folly has lost her? Oh, that I might die! that I might die!" And, sobbing like a child, he falls upon his knees before the pitying, compassionate face of his friend.

"Come, Charteris," says Sir Edward, "be a man—bear it bravely. We all have our troubles, Heaven knows! I too have a heavy burden to bear, and I feel often as if it were beyond my strength."

'" But, oh, think of mine, think of mine ! ' moans the wretched, broken-down man before him. "And to know that I owe it all to—"

Quite suddenly he springs to his feet. His face is ghastly pale, his burning eyes look wildly before him.

"I forgot," he says. "Ha, ha ! I make but a sorry bridegroom, do I not, Llewellyn ? Let me make amends at last. You shall come with me and be introduced to—my wife ! "

He makes one step forward towards the door ; but ere he reaches it, he throws his arms wildly forward and falls to the ground as senseless and helpless as the dead.

CHAPTER II.

 FORTNIGHT has passed since Yolande was taken ill, and to-day she has been pronounced out of danger. Save for extreme weakness, and a slight irritating cough that comes on in the evenings, she feels " as well as ever," so she says. But the doctor never ceases to impress upon her and all around her the necessity of extreme care, and the advisability of trying a warmer climate for the winter.

She is lying on a couch in the dressing-room adjoining her bedroom, for this is the first day she has been able to get up, and Rose Bertram sits beside her. She keeps her face studiously averted from Yolande, for it is a very tell-tale face, and the anxiety depicted upon it at the present time might have struck any casual observer.

" I am sure you must be tired of me, dear Rose," says the invalid, softly. " What a trouble I have been to you all this time, and how good and patient you were ! I wonder you are not worn out ! But Enid is coming to-morrow, and so you will be relieved. How kind it was of Sir Edward to go and fetch her ! "

For Yolande knows nothing of the real cause of the master of Llewellyn's absence, nor how for three days and nights he has watched beside the couch of the man who was once his rival. Doctor Deane declares that Charteris has had a narrow escape of brain fever, and that nothing but his friend's incessant care has warded it off. However, a heart-sick, grey, haggard man rises from the three days' couch of agony and delirium, and, looking up at the face of the man who has saved him, cries passionately, " Could you not even let me die ? "

It is but poor thanks to receive for the self-sacrifice entailed, but Sir Edward feels only pity, not anger, and says compassionately,—

"Life and death are not in man's hands, Charteris. You have work yet to do in the world, be sure of that."

But of all this Yolande knows nothing. Lying pale and shadowy on her couch, she thinks remorsefully of her cold letter to Denzil· Her doubts begin to die away. She remembers the proud, imperious, love-lit face where truth spoke out in every line. She remembers his words, so tender, so loving, so sad. She asks herself is it possible that one short week would have changed him so ? She even makes excuses for the tone of his letter. He may have been worried, pressed for time, puzzled by difficulties. Why should she have condemned him so readily ? In her weakness, and thankfulness for the life that has been spared, her pride gives way, her heart softens.

"Rose," she says, presently, " do you know if any one wrote to Mr Charteris about my illness ? "

" No, Mrs Davies forgot ; and she was the
only one who knew his address," answers the
girl.

" Ah, then he does not know ? " Yolande
cries, eagerly, the bright pink spot which ex-
citement always brings into her cheeks now
burning brighter and deeper as she raises herself to a sitting position. " Rose, dear, I must
write to him at once. He will think it so
strange, all this silence."

" No, Yolande—not yet. You are too
weak," urges Rose, earnestly. " Wait a few
days more, dear, till you are stronger and
more like yourself. Perhaps he is on his
way here even now. He might come back
at any moment."

Yolande smiles ; such a tender, wistful smile
that it makes her friend's heart ache as she
sees it.

" At any time, on any day ! " she echoes,
softly. " How nice and comforting that
sounds, Rose ! Oh, I do hope he will ! You
know, dear, we had a little—not quarrel—

difference, and I was very proud and cold
about it, and wrote him an angry letter.
How I wish I had not done it now! I
suppose," she adds, wistfully, "there is no
other from him? Nothing came since I
have been ill?"

"No," says Rose, bending over the fire
and intently arranging an obstinate coal that
seems very unequally balanced.

Yolande sighs. She feels disappointed, but
still bravely tries to repress it, and tells herself that it is all her own fault.

"I think I ought to write," she says again,
gently but decidedly. "Come Rose, darling,
be good and hand me my desk from the
table there. I will send only two or three
lines, I promise you."

Rose is in despair. She knows the whole sad,
pitiful tale. She knows that the fragile, loving
girl beside her has no right now to address as
a lover the man who is lost to her for ever.
Yet what can she do? To deny, or excuse,
will only arouse suspicion. Perhaps it is

better to let her have her way. She brings
the desk and puts it on a small table beside
the couch, and arranges th pillows behind
Yolande, so that she may lean back even
while writing. The grateful smile and ear-
nest kiss she receives as thanks, almost break
down her composure. She feels a lump in
her throat, a sudden dimness comes into her
eyes, as she turns away hurriedly.

Yolande is sitting up now, and the position
shows her the reflection of herself in the large
mirror opposite to her couch.

" I did not think I looked so well, Rose,"
she says, brightly. " Why, I have as much
colour as ever, haven't I ? Of course I am
thinner "—and she looks at the slender white
arms for which the sleeves of her dressing-
gown seem so unaccountably large —" decidedly thinner," she goes on, seeing how
loosely the once well-fitting robe hangs around
her pretty figure. " Like poor love-lorn
Glorvina, I must have ' me frocks tuk in.'
But I daresay I shall soon get plump again,

once I can leave the house and get about. I shall have to drink Guinness's stout, the double X—sha'n't I, Rose ?—or cod liver oil, or something of that kind. I don't like to be thin, you know. Don't you remember how we laughed at Jane Croft when she said no waist could be genteel that measured over twenty inches ? I suppose mine is genteel by this time ! "

So, babbling on with foolish, merry words, she begins her letter, while Rose Bertram kneels by the fire in an agony of dread and shame, marvelling how the poor, trusting, ignorant girl will receive the awful news in store for her.

It is not a very long letter that Yolande writes, but a sweet, trusting, tender little letter, every sentence of which will burn in words of fire to the heart of the man who reads it. She tells him that she has had only one letter from him, and that that was so strangely cold and unloverlike that it made her angry, and so called forth the

abrupt and equally cold response. Then she
speaks of her accident and illness, and finally
tells him how she longs to see him again
—how in her weakness and weariness her
heart calls always and only for him, and,
if he can come, or cares to come, how gladly
she will welcome him after these weeks of
absence and restraint.

" There," she says, after it is signed, sealed,
and addressed; " now I feel better. You
must please put it into the post-bag yourself,
Rose, and I shall know it is safe."

And so thankful is Rose for the excuse to
leave the room that she hurries off with most
suspicious alacrity. On the way she stops at
Miss Llewellyn's door.

" Please go and sit with her a little while,"
she entreats. " To have to stop there and
hear her talk in all her innocence and uncon-
sciousness is more than I can bear." And
she bursts into bitter agonised weeping.

The kind old maiden lady soothes her very
gently, and then, bidding her remain quiet

until she has recovered her usual composure, she hurries away to the invalid's room.

"And so you are really up again, my dear!" she says, brightly, as Yolande rises from her recumbent attitude to greet her.

"Yes, and feeling so much better and stronger," the girl answers, joyfully. "Don't you think I got over it well?"

"Wonderfully," is the hearty rejoinder; and Miss Llewellyn bends over the girl, kissing her many times, and wraps the white fleecy shawl more closely round the slender figure.

"You did not think I should be well so soon, did you?" persists Yolande, cheerfully. "The doctor says I must have a good constitution."

"Yes," says the old lady, calmly, wondering what it is in the look and aspect of the beautiful girl which sends so sharp a thrill of pain to her compassionate heart. But she is accustomed to rigid self-control, and Yolande cannot see the effort it costs her to look and speak in her usual manner.

Miss Llewellyn sits quietly chatting to the sick girl upon a thousand light indifferent matters—of her sister's expected arrival, of the near approach of Christmas, of Rose Bertram's regret at being obliged to go back to school for the last three weeks of the term —of anything and everything that can amuse and distract her fancy for the moment, until at last Yolande, with a little tired sigh, declares she is lazy enough to long for bed ; and Rose is summoned, and they both undress her, and the couch is wheeled back with her on it, and once more she nestles among the downy pillows, and closes her eyes, declaring after all she cannot be quite so strong as she thought she was.

All this is heart-rending to Rose ; and all the time she dreads what the future only too surely has in store for the sorely-tired girl. She has to smile and move about, and decry Yolande's languid fears, and tell her she will soon be strong and well once more, only she must not expect too much at once.

Enid Mervyn arrives next day, and is shocked at the change in her sister. Not being accustomed to self-control, she gives way, despite all Miss Llewellyn's cautions, to bitter weeping and lamentations at sight of Yolande. Rose is very wroth with her, and declares sternly that she will not leave her in charge of her patient if she is going to behave in such a silly, childish way. At this Enid gets indignant. She is sixteen now, and quite as tall as Yolande, though angular and undeveloped in comparison with her sister's exquisitely-proportioned figure. But she is very pretty—almost as pretty as Yolande, Sir Edward Llewellyn thinks. She has the same wavy, curly hair, though more brown than gold lurks in its brightness, and her eyes are brown and soft as a water-brook that runs over dark dim pebbles underneath the shadows of thick-foliaged trees.

Such eyes are very fascinating ; sparkling, tender, soft, beseeching, capable of mirroring every motion, from laughter to sorrow, from pity to pain; and they have been brought to play upon the lacerated feelings of the handsome young baronet in a way which shows Enid too is not quite inexperienced in those witching arts that seemed so peculiarly to belong to "My Lady Coquette."

At Rose Bertram's rebuke she stifles back the sobs that have so distressed Yolande, and begins, with all the composure and alacrity that Rose herself has displayed, to render her sister the little services she still requires.

Sir Edward has been obliged to explain to Enid the state of affairs between Denzil and Yolande, and has sternly impressed upon her the need of caution in mentioning his name if her sister should speak of him.

"As soon as she is stronger the truth must be told," he says, very sadly; "but that lies between Charteris and herself. Heaven pity them in the ordeal! What we have to do is to get up her strength as fast as we can, so that the shock may not fall on a weakened frame. Even with all that care and affection can do, I dread the result inexpressibly."

Something in his voice and face makes the quick-witted girl look up sharply.

" So that's how the land lies!" she says to herself. "Yolande has been at her old tricks! Will she ever be able to spare a single man she comes across?"

She promises to be discretion itself, however, and fulfils her promise fairly well, telling Yolande that Denzil Charteris is as busy as he can be with following up the hue-and-cry after the supposed murderer of the unknown man found drowned in Dead Man's Pool.

"And he has been ill too," she says, foolishly.

"Ill!"—and Yolande turns deadly pale. "Oh, and I was so cruel, and thought such hard things of him!" And thereto she falls into such an agony of remorse that Enid sorely regrets her inadvertence.

For the next few days every drop of

nourishment and medicine the invalid takes is coaxed down with Denzil's name, and the declaration what a pleasure it would be to him to see her strong and like herself. But the best and most miraculous medicine of all is a paper, bearing a few blotted lines of hurried writing. It only says,—

" MY DARLING,—Get well and strong as fast as you can. When you are better I will be with you. I only await the doctor's permission."

After that there is nothing the girl will not take so that only she may get better. It is nothing short of marvellous the rapid strides she makes now. She wants to get well. Her whole heart and mind is bent on achieving this one object—and that is half the battle.

So another week goes by ; and now Yolande can walk by herself from room to room on the same floor. She does not need to be lifted on her pillows or trouble other people to fetch and carry for her. Fortunately too the weather is unusually mild, and there are no chilling winds and bitter blasts to tell upon her delicate frame. Still every one has so strongly counselled her going to Italy for the winter that at last she consents to do so.

" We will all go," she says to Enid—" the dear old dad too ; and Skippy shall chaperon and look after us—eh, Enid ? And, perhaps, if Denzil is not going to be very busy, and all this horrible law-business is settled soon, he will be able to come too. He has travelled so much, and knows all about foreign ways and tongues. What fun it would be ! "

Poor Enid turns faint at the thought of the misery in store for the happy, trusting girl. Every day the fear grows deeper in the minds of all who watch and tend her, that the impending blow which is bound to fall on her joyful anticipations, will be more than her strength can bear.

" It seems so wrong, so shameful to let her go on believing all she does ! " cries Enid, passionately, to Sir Edward, as they stand before the drawing-room fire a fortnight after her arrival at the Hall.

"But what can we do?" he asks in bewilderment. "She must know all or nothing. This is no case for half measures. Her health is the first and most important consideration, is it not?"

"Of course," answers the girl, gazing sorrowfully into the glowing embers at her feet. "But it is terribly hard to have to hear her innocent questions and remarks, and all her plans and projects for the future, and know all the time— Oh, Heaven, why did she ever care for that man?" she breaks off suddenly. "He has caused her nothing but misery from the first, and yet she is absolutely infatuated! I cannot understand it."

"Love is not in our hands to give or control," says Sir Edward, sadly. "If it were, how different the world would be!"

"Yes; but even then two or three might give it to the same person," answers Enid, a little mischievously. "Look at Yolande, for instance. I'm sure, ever since she was a child in short frocks, every male being who has come near her has fallen in love with her! It's positively dreadful, for she can't marry every·one ; can she ? "

"Certainly not," he says, with a faint smile. "But, as you must allow, the men cannot be blamed for succumbing to her fascinations."

"I'm sure I wish she'd give me some ! " remarks Enid, dolefully. "It's too bad that one member of the family should have all the attractions ! Now I and my other sister are as different as possible from her."

"Perhaps that is just as well," says S ir Edward. "Fancy three such sirens in a family ! What would become of the men in your county ? "

Enid laughs.

"Oh, they could take very good care of themselves, I'm sure ! " she answers. "Sir Edward "—and her voice grows grave again—

"do you know if it is really true that Mrs Charteris has left her husband?"

"Yes," he says; and he too looks pale and disturbed now. "She left Beechhampton on the day he was pronounced out of danger. You know even in his worst moments she was not allowed to approach him. He seemed to feel her presence, and it drove him into a fresh paroxysm. At last Doctor Deane forbade her to come near the room."

"And do you know where she went?" asks Enid, pityingly.

"No; she left no word or message. It was supposed she had gone to her mother. Charteris himself has never mentioned her name since."

"Poor fellow! It must be awful for him," says Enid, her voice full of intense compassion. "Only fancy finding himself married to the woman who had tricked and deluded him so skilfully! I can't imagine how it all came about even yet. Of course no one knew anything about the matter until the announcement appeared in the papers. We could hardly believe it even then."

"They were married by special licence," says Sir Edward. "I can't think how Charteris could have been such a fool. But there—I must not speak ill of the poor fellow. He has suffered terribly enough for his credulity. She must have laid her schemes very skilfully indeed to have succeeded so well."

"You have not yet discovered who sent that notice to the paper here?" asks Enid, gazing thoughtfully at the clouded, sorrowful face of the young man.

"No," he says. "I can do nothing, because I know no friends or enemies of your sister; and that newspaper paragraph is part of a deep-laid scheme, which she alone can help us to fathom. That woman did her work very well, I must say."

"Ah, well, she will have her reward," observes Enid. "She cannot expect to have any honest regard from man or woman now.

Her husband will not live with her, and so the very object for which she schemed is defeated. I almost wonder he did not murder her, in his rage and shame, when he first discovered her treachery. The Charteris race are fearfully passionate and fearfully proud."

" I almost feared he would at first," says Sir Edward, wondering a little whether these are quite suitable topics for a young girl to discuss, and yet not seeing how he can avoid such discussion.

"And what will become of her, do you suppose?" asks Enid, after a long thoughtful pause.

" I—I really cannot imagine," he says, rousing himself with a faint start.

"What would you do in such a case?" inquires the girl, regarding him curiously.

"I?" he says—and his voice grows stern with repressed pain. " I could never be in such a case, Miss Enid, for the testimony of the whole world would have weighed nothing in my mind against your sister's simple word. Unless she herself had stood before me, and then and there declared her perfidy, I should never have believed ill of her."

" O-h ! " says Enid, looking with reluctant admiration at the splendid truth and constancy of the noble face. " What a pity she did not care for—you ! "

He flushes to the very roots of his hair ; and she, seeing the flush, repents swiftly of the ill-advised words. Her eyes droop in confusion.

" I beg your pardon," she stammers. " I did not mean to pain you. I—I am always so accustomed to speak out what I think, that I forgot."

" There is nothing to pardon," he says, gently, as he looks at the pretty blushing face and soft troubled eyes, and feels his heart beat faster even at the transient resemblance they bear to another face and another pair of eyes. " You are too honest not to speak out what you think ; and I honour you for it. Besides, why should I

seek to deny it ?   I did care for your sister.
I do still, though I know it is utterly, absolutely hopeless.   But, for all that, I am not
going to pass my life in repining at the fate
that has given her love far enough away
from me.   I would rather put her happiness
before my own, and, if anything I could do
would further it, I should never grudge any
pain to myself—never !"

"How good you are!" says Enid, softly ;
and the soft words comfort him strangely,
not only now, but in many a day to come,
when they float back with his memory of
this hour.

CHAPTER III.

" T is most extraordinary," says Mr Herrick, as he paces the dreary gravel walks of his dreary garden one cold November day — "most extraordinary ! "

He shakes his head and buttons his long coat more closely round his long spare frame, gazing all the time with thoughtful eyes at the ground at his feet, as if it held the clue to the problem he was solving.

He raises his head sharply enough however as a footstep sounds behind him, and, facing round, he takes in, with one brief comprehensive glance, the aspect and features of the advancing stranger.

There is nothing very remarkable about the

man. He is slight, pale, quiet-looking, and
plainly dressed in dark clothes—not a work-
ing-man or a tradesman evidently ; and yet it
would puzzle any one to assign him a position
higher than the one or lower than the other.

" Good morning, sir," he says, touching his
hat. " Mr Herrick, I believe ? "

" Yes," answers the lawyer, curtly. " And
you ? "

" I come from Mr Lancaster, sir," the man
says, quietly. " He said you wanted an under-
gardener."

" Exactly," answers the lawyer, with a grim
smile. " From all Mr Lancaster said, you
ought to suit the place exactly."

" I hope to do so, sir," says the man, with
due humility and a business-like composure
of manner.

The lawyer chuckles for a moment ; but his
mirth has no more effect upon the quiet im-
perturbable being before him than if he had
been merely a piece of carved wood.

" Ha, ha ! You'll do—you'll do ! " says Mr

Herrick, when his merriment has evaporated. " Come — you mustn't look so suspicious ; there's not a soul to hear us. I've sent my man to the village, and my old woman is as deaf as a post. Now to business. Any clue yet ? "

" I can't say there is, sir."

" Humph ! Well, I hardly expected it so soon. Now, Mr— What's your name, by the way ? "

" James Dowling, sir.'

" Dowling, then. Well, look here. I've a special interest in this matter ; and, though I've given up practising for many years, I mean to have a try at my old game again. It's a queer hole-and-corner case this, for we can't get at who the murdered man is, in the first place ; in the next, the only witness who saw the crime committed is dead ; but we have her confession, so that's something to go by. As for the man suspected, he's dropped clean out of sight. He bolted to London the moment Mr Charteris turned up—gave up his situation in the police force and disappeared. From that hour to this no one has seen or heard anything of him.   Humph !   Why, what are you smiling at ? "

It could hardly be called a smile, the faint quiver at the corner of the mouth, fading into gravity as soon as noticed.

" Nothing, sir," is the quiet rejoinder. " Only I was thinking of one of the queerest cases I ever had, where the fellow had given us all the slip, and we were sure he had gone to America.   One of our men even was clever enough to discover the vessel, and slipped on board and made a capture quite with stage effect—only of the wrong man."

" Well," asks Mr Herrick, impatiently.

" Well, sir, all the time the real criminal was living quietly and working within a few miles of the spot where the murder had been committed.   He was so well disguised no one knew him.

" And was he caught at last ? " inquires the lawyer, growing interested.

" He was, sir, and by your humble servant."

" You did it, then ? " exclaims Mr Herrick, with interest. " Will you tell me how ? "

" Yes, sir ; for it was curious how I found him out. His very mother and sisters never recognised him. Even his voice was changed. I was sent to make inquiries down at the place, and, strange to say, this man was the first person I tackled. He had it all so per- fectly—the means, the motives, the flight of the criminal—that somehow, I cannot tell why, I grew suspicious of him. Still he was so awfully cautious that I was two months dodging about, and yet as far off as ever from discovering the truth. He never drank, so there was no chance of unloosing his tongue that way. He always slept alone, and al- ways with his door locked. He riled me so that once I almost thought of turning in- cendiarist and setting his cottage on fire, so as to see if he forgot his disguise in the alarm of the moment. But that was too great a risk for me. So at last I gave out that we had found a clue, and that the real murderer was in London. The next day I left the place, returning in a new disguise by the night train. I went to the cottage. It was all dark, save one window belonging to his sleeping-room ; and there I had noticed before a light had always burned, though he carefully shuttered the window so that no outsider might see it. The cottage was low, and I easily climbed up by means of a gardening ladder. There was just one chink through which the light shone. While I had my eyes on it the shutters were suddenly thrown open from the inside, revealing the room. I had hardly time to scramble down and hide myself in the bushes near by, when the man unfastened the window, and, to my amazement, got out."

" Did he not wonder at finding the ladder there ? " asks Mr Herrick.

" He might have done so at another time," says the man. " But you see, sir, he was asleep."

" Asleep ! " echoes the lawyer, in surprise.

"Asleep as sound as a door-nail," is the answer. " Of course I didn't know at first, for it was too dark to see his face; but I followed him as quiet as I could, and he led me—where do you think, sir ? "

" Not to the place ? " hazards Mr Herrick.

" There, and nowhere else," returns the man—" as straight as he could go."

" And what did you do ? " asks the lawyer.

" Followed him, and saw him go through the wretched pantomime in his sleep, which in his waking moments had made him a murderer," answers the detective, slowly. " I'm not a man given to squeamishness, sir ; it don't do for us, otherwise we should never keep our places. But I will confess that the sight of that wretched being drawn back by some resistless force to the very place he had hitherto avoided, and there, with his brain locked in sleep, making full confession of his long-guarded secret, did give me the queerest turn I've ever known. I went up at last, and touched him on the arm. He woke; and to my dying day I shall never forget the scream of horror that left his lips. He hurled himself at me like a madman; and he was a strong man too, and desperate. It was hard work to get him under, but I did it at last; and, though I had neither warrant nor anything else to give me the lawful right to capture him, I just clapped the irons on his wrists, and told him he might as well make a clean breast of it, for I'd every proof of his guilt."

" And did he confess ? "

" Yes, sir; and I had all the credit of as neat a capture as could be desired. It gave me a great rise did that little case. I always call it the case of the sleep-walker."

" Well, I wish you may be as successful in the present instance," says the lawyer, gravely. " But the man I suspect is too cunning and cool a villain to give us such a loop-hole as your sleep-walker did."

" Yes, he's another sort of chap altogether,"

answers the detective. "Still, in every case
of murder—with but rare exceptions—there's
always something done or left undone to
convict the criminal. It's a mercy that it
is so. It's not a very noble or edifying thing
to have to resort to all kinds of mean ex-
pedients to entrap our fellow-men, is it, sir?
I used to think so myself at first; but I've
got hardened now. I think it's only fair to
meet treachery by treachery, cunning by
cunning. The instruments which the murderer uses against his victim are turned
against himself. Yes; I think now, if ever
there was a case where the end justifies the
means, it is that of hunting a criminal to
justice."

"I agree with you," says Mr Herrick.
"Heavens! what a state of life and society
there would be if murderers and thieves
stalked red-handed among us, laughing with
impunity at every effort to convict them,
triumphing in the vile skill that enables them
to evade all pursuit and accusation! The

detective force is one of the greatest boons to all classes, the innocent as well as the guilty."

" But now, sir," suggests the detective, " let us proceed to the business we have in view. There is a reward of fifty pounds offered for any information respecting the man who was murdered, and a further reward of one hundred pounds to the discoverer of the murderer. Is it not so ? "

" Yes. And Mr Lancaster recommended you to me as being specially suited to what I call a ' blind ' case. I have told you whom I consider the criminal. The description in Mrs Charteris's confession tallies exactly with Budd ; but not knowing the reason of the crime and the impossibility of identifying the murdered man, make it very difficult to discover anything. It may have been revenge or robbery. It may have been a hot quarrel that resulted in the blow that struck him down into the water. We have nothing tangible to hold to."

"I want a full description of the man first, sir," remarks the detective. "I suppose there's not such a thing as a picture of him to be got anywhere?"

"I fear not," says Mr Herrick. He was not a man given to personal vanity. But come along with me into my study now, and I will tell you all about his physiognomy, as far as personal description can do it."

"You won't forget, sir," suggests the man, respectfully, "that I'm only your under-gardener for the time?"

"No, I sha'n't forget," chuckles the old lawyer, grimly—"an idle, lazy, good-for-nothing sort of chap, a deal too fond of loitering in the village, and drinking and gossiping with the folk around—eh, Dowling?"

"If you please, sir."

"If I please! Ha, ha! Well, come along, come along! My old servant is in the kitchen, and won't see us go into the house. I suppose you'll want to change your toggery by-and-by, eh?"

" Yes, sir.   I have got all that."

" Humph !   That's right."   And, with no further observation, Mr Herrick leads the way into the gloomy old house, the detective quietly following.

CHAPTER IV.

"ENID, how do I look? Not very dreadful, do I?" asks Yolande.

"Not at all dreadful," says Enid, with a suppressed sigh, as she thinks that in an hour more her sister will care little enough for the appearance which now she is making as fair as fair can be for her lover's eyes.

"He will be here so soon now," continues the happy girl. "It does not seem so long ago since we parted, when I look back to-day, though it has been terribly long to bear. But I am glad you made me wait till I was well before you sent for him, because now he won't think me so much altered. I am paler than I used to be, am I not, Enid? But am I very much thinner, do you think?"

"Oh, Yolande," cries the girl, wildly, "why do you trouble about such things? Don't you know it's you yourself Denzil cares about? He won't think of anything else."

"Oh, but he will—after a time!" says Yolande, with her old lovely blush. "He will take note of every change in face and form. I know him better than you do, Enid. I wish my heart would not beat so fast," she goes on agitatedly. "And just look at the absurd way my hand trembles! I have run this pin three times into my neck instead of into my frill. Please do it for me, Enid. Why, how pale you look, dear! You have no need to be agitated, I'm sure."

"I know," she responds, shivering involuntarily. "I am cold, Yolande; that is all."

"Cold? And in that thick dress?" says Yolande. "Well, my dear, you had better run down to the library; there is always a good fire there. It is so kind of Miss Llewellyn to give up her lovely little boudoir to—us." Again the soft shy blush crimsons her delicate cheeks. "You will see he comes up at once, Enid, won't you? I can't stand waiting as I used to do. I am not quite strong yet, you know."

Every word stabs poor Enid to the heart and taxes her self-control to the uttermost. Again and again does some trembling word of warning or preparation rise to her lips; but again and again is it forced back. She has been sternly forbidden to say anything. Only Denzil Charteris himself is to tell the girl he loves, the sad, pitiful tale of treachery and wrong.

"I haven't put on any finery," Yolande continues, looking at the reflection of the slight pretty figure in its dress of navy-blue serge, the lace ruffles at throat and wrist its only relief. "Finery doesn't suit an invalid, Enid. Do you know I never coughed once all last night? I believe if only the wind never went to the east I should be as well as you are."

"Let's hope it never blows from that

quarter in Italy," answers Enid, who is standing by the window now, looking with straining eyes for the approaching carriage.

"Let us hope so indeed," echoes Yolande, giving a last touch to the lovely shining locks that wave and curl in nature's own luxuriant fashion over her dainty little head. "We shall go off there as soon as ever I am able to travel, Enid. And I shall take such care of the dear old man at home that perhaps the change of air and scene may do him good too. What a mercy it is, Enid, that all this time he has never missed me! I could never have left home had he been as he was before."

"You gave us all a terrible fright, running off as you did," says Enid, "and then posting your letters in London, and never giving any address to write to. Really, now I come to think of it, your whole course of conduct looked uncommonly guilty."

"I can't help that," she answers, shuddering even now at the recollection of that

terrible time. " Do you know, Enid, I never
quite believed Denzil was dead even then ?
I felt as if I should know and feel the reality
of his death had it really happened. And
when, after all that dreadful time, I saw him
one evening — without any warning — walk
into the rectory drawing-room here, I felt
more relief than surprise, frightened as I
was."

" I wonder you did not take him for a
ghost," says Enid, marvelling how the conversation always turns back to that one
subject, try as she may to avoid it.

A little happy laugh leaves Yolande's lips.

" No," she says. " He did not look at all
ghostly. I wonder if he is much changed
now ? He has been ill too, poor darling ! Ah,
I have been so wretched since he left me ! I
did not think it could have made such a
difference in my life—just his absence. I
don't think I shall ever try the experiment of
another parting. We must always be together
now, until—"

But Enid can bear it no longer.

" Oh, Yolande," she cries, wildly, don't think so much of him—don't ! Have you not other people to love you and to love ? Is all the world nothing beside this one man ? "

Yolande looks wonderingly at the pale trembling young face.

" It is not that I love any of you less, dear," she says, softly ; " but he— Ah, well, some day you too will understand ! "

"Shall I ? " questions Enid, dreamily, as with a choking sob she turns away once more. " Almost I could hope—not."

" There are the wheels ! " cries Yolande, turning white as death in the great eagerness and agitation of the moment. " Quick, Enid darling ; run down and meet him ! No, don't stay to help me. I can walk these few steps quite well."

She moves away swiftly to the warm cosy boudoir, the room where the most terrible scene in her life's drama is to be enacted ; the room, the memory of which henceforth will fill her with sharpest pain as she thinks of the agony it witnessed.

But as yet she knows nothing. She leans against the couch, her hand on its back, as if to gain some slight support. Her heart seems to stand still ; her whole being is absorbed in the one intensity of listening, listening for the music of the returning step, so long silent, listening for the sound of the tender voice for which her ears are aching. Every pulse pauses, then throbs in wild, mad unison. He is coming ; he is close at hand ; he is here !

The door opens, and even in the glad rapture that thrills her to the very core and centre of her being there comes some strange chill touch of pain. He is so sadly, strangely changed !

All the welcomes she has framed, all the pretty tender sentences that she has rehearsed so glibly, are utterly forgotten now. One thing only she sees—his arms outstretched as in by-gone days. That is enough. With a low faint cry of inexpressible happiness she flutters birdlike into that close embrace, while between them no word is spoken, no question asked. There is only a great silence.

She would fain raise her head at last ; but he presses it down against his breast, and the great fierce throbs of his heart frighten her as they sound upon her ear.

" Oh, Denzil," she says, softly, " I have been so ill, so miserable ! Why did you try me so ? Did you want to find out if I loved you really ? Oh, my darling, I did—so dearly ! "

Her voice breaks into a little sob, but he makes no answer ; the laboured throbs of the poor suffering heart grow duller, slower, more painful.

" You have been ill too, poor fellow ! " she goes on, pityingly, trying to raise her head so as to look into the well-beloved face once more.

What is it that curdles her warm young blood with such an icy fear, that stays the words on her pale lips, and leaves her gazing

mutely at him now with such an anguish in
the dumb and sorrowful eyes, as never any
woe or pain has brought into them before ?

" Denzil," she implores, " tell me—are you
ill, or—has something happened ? "

She cannot shape the vague fear at her
heart into anything tangible yet. At those
words he unfolds his arms and places her
gently on the couch.

" Yes," he says—and his voice is altogether
strange and harsh and full of a soul-wrung
agony, that makes the girl tremble—" something—has happened ! "

No sound breaks the awful pause that
follows those brief words. They stand and
look at each other. Then a great calmness
steals over Yolande. She puts out her hand
—it does not even tremble.

" Sit down here," she says, " and tell
me."

But, instead of obeying her, he throws himself at her feet and buries his face in her lap,
trembling from head to foot with a strong

man's agony ; kneeling thus, in a few brief words he tells her all.

She does not weep, or moan, or utter any sound ; but, as the last word leaves his lips, and she feels the scalding touch of tears on her hands—tears wrung from the innermost depths of his heart, and for which he feels no shame and she no wonder—her icy calm gives way. She lowers her head to his, noting even in that moment of horrible torture the grey hairs that streak its dark rich curls. How is it she has never seen them before ?

" Oh, my poor Denzil ! " she says.

That is all. There is no blame for him, no pity for herself for all the long, blank, dreary years that stretch before her. Her eyes are quite dry. A little while ago she could have wept ; but then her heart was all unstrung and quivering with every breath of emotion. Now—ah, now ? Is this cold dead weight within her bosom a heart at all ? she wonders.

" Won't you look at me, Denzil ? " she says

at last. "We must part soon now, and I have hardly seen your face once. I suppose it is not wrong to want to say farewell to it ? Not so very long ago it was mine, and after to-day—"

He looks up ; the little tender break in the pretty wistful voice recalls him to himself. She gazes at the noble, passionate features, from which all the life and glow have faded, leaving only a haggard-worn reflection of all that she remembers.

"How I have looked forward to our meeting!" she says, shivering. "And now I suppose even that is a wrong to your—wife !"

"For Heaven's sake do not you pollute that name by giving it to the traitress who has murdered our every hope of happiness !" he cries, with such a fire of fury blazing in his eyes as frightens her for a moment. "Yolande, you only are my wife in Heaven's sight. No other woman can bear that title while you live."

"Hush !" she says, and lays one cold little hand against his fevered lips. "Denzil, you

have lost all right to say such words to me.
Wrong or sinful as she is, bitterly as she has
made us both regard her, yet none the less
she is bound to you by every human law.
She bears your name, she holds your honour.
Did you not vow yourself to her as long as
you both shall live ? "

He springs hastily to his feet, and his voice
rings out with bitter scorn.

" As long as I live," he cries, fiercely, " she
may bear my name ; but she shall be no
more to me than the veriest stranger who
passes me in the street ! "

Yolande's heart gives one throb of guilty
joy. Does he mean it ? she thinks. Is the
woman who has duped and wronged them to
be punished thus ? Has she no need to fear
that wonderful rival's beauty blinding his
senses till he forgets even her wrong-doing
for the sake of her love and her loveliness ?
Will she indeed be banished from his presence, receiving no kiss, no word, no caress,
that are denied herself ?   It were fitting

punishment, if she loves him with one-tenth part of the love crushing this poor weak girl's heart, if she has sinned and laboured and schemed so long only to find her reward in his life-long abhorrence and neglect. But a moment after this harsh revengeful tide of passion and despair sweeps on, and leaves her trembling at her own baseness.

"I am growing wicked too," she thinks. "Come here, Denzil," she says, softly. "I am not strong yet, and I cannot bear this much longer. Dear, it almost breaks my heart to have to say 'Good-bye' to you again; and yet I must say it. I had planned such a merry, happy time for us. I thought you too might come to Italy when I went, and see how much better I grew, and rejoice with me over the returning health that brought me nearer to— But no—I must not say that. Oh, Denzil, how hard it is to keep off that one topic!"

"Oh, Yolande, your words kill me!" he groans.

"No, no," she says, hurriedly; "you are
brave and strong, dear. You will not give
way even beneath this heavy yoke; for you
must do your duty, Denzil, hard as it is. A
few months ago, when I was only a giddy,
thoughtless girl, I do not think I could have
borne to tell you this; but since I have been
ill I have looked at things with different eyes,
and I know that Heaven's blessing sometimes
come to us in different shapes from what we
desire or expect. Your duty, Denzil, is to
return to your wife; for she is your wife,
say what you will, and you are bound
to try and be true and good to her, even
though you do not love her as—as you love
me."

"I hate her!" he cries, hoarsely. "How
little you know of men, you poor little child,
when you give me such counsel as this!
Why, do you know that to see her at my
table in the place I pictured you, her figure in
each spot and nook where yours has lived for
me in every thought of wife, her head laid

where yours should lie—great Heaven, it maddens me to think of it ! "

" You gave her my place, Denzil," says the sweet low voice. " You married her."

" True ! But I was not sane or reasonable. She bewitched and deluded me by arts that fitted in cunningly with the reaction of my wrongs, dealt, as I thought, by your hands. Oh, my love, my little sweetheart, bid me do anything, however hard—bid me go from you to misery, madness, despair — but do not bid me take that traitress to my home again ! It is a task beyond my strength ! "

" And have you thought of the questions that will be asked ? " she says, still calmly. " Have you thought what reason you can give to the world for thus casting adrift the woman who is of your blood, your race, and to whom you have given your name ? "

" I care nothing for the world or the babbling tongues of the fools around," he answers, gloomily. " If it be your will that she comes to Beechhampton, I leave. The same roof can never shelter her and me ! "

" She too loves you," pleads the girl.

" Love ! "—and his scornful laugh cuts like a lash. " A fine love, to mock and fool me, to ruin my happiness and yours, to wrest by force of cunning what she could never obtain by right or honest means ! Yolande, do not pollute the name thus ! "

She sits quite silent, too weak to urge another plea, yet bravely trying to stifle the sinful pleasure at her heart.

" She is a weak and erring woman, Denzil," she falters slowly ; "but, oh, my dear, can you not forgive her ? She will have to suffer more than you could. Leave her punishment in Heaven's hands."

" If you loved me," he says, passionately, " you would never send me back to her ? You would bid me put seas and lands between us both ; for in very truth, Yolande, such a woman may tempt me to—murder ! "

" Oh, no—oh, no ! " she wails. " It is not

you who are speaking now, Denzil. It is some
evil spirit striving to master your better
reason. Look—I am only a weak girl, and I
have loved you with all the force of my whole
heart—I can give no other man a thought or
feeling that has once been yours; and I see
this woman step between us, and turn to sin
our love that was so pure and beautiful, and
place herself between your heart and mine,
and wave me back from your side by right of
plighted vows that make her sacred ; and yet
I can bid you go, because—oh, Denzil, because
surely duty is higher than even love ! And
after all life is not so very, very long ; and the
reward of suffering here is all to come—hereafter ! Do you not believe this, Denzil ? "

" No," he says, gloomily. " I only know I
have lost you. And, if you loved as I love,
you would have room for no other thought.
Can any good hereafter atone for the loss of
all that makes life sweet and fair ? I do not
believe it ! "

" Yes, you do—you must," the girl cries,

passionately ; " for, oh, Denzil, parted as we
are here, what comfort is there for you or
me if we cannot look forward to—that other
meeting ? "

He looks at her, all his soul in his pleading
eyes, the pale, careworn misery of his face
taxing her self-command to the utmost. A
wild impulse crosses her mind to throw herself into his arms, to bid him do what he
likes with her, so that only they two are
together, defying the world, but happy even
in that defiance ; but only for a moment does
that fierce temptation last. She thrusts it
sharply, swiftly aside, but her face pales to
the hue of his own, and great tears gather
slowly in her eyes.

" My love," he says, mournfully, and kneels
beside her once more, pressing his hot lips
on the cold and trembling hands that lie so
tightly clasped in her lap, " my own little
sweetheart, what can I say, what can I do
to comfort you ? The love of my whole heart
is yours so utterly and entirely that I have

no thought, no hope apart from you. When I thought you were false, I went mad with the shame and shock. I do not remember one sane or painless hour till I awoke from a dream of agony and saw the man I thought your lover stand before me saying, ' It is a lie—all ! ' "

" And it was too late then ? " asks Yolande, bitterly. " You—you were married ? "

" Heaven forgive me—yes ! "

A strange bright streak of colour comes into the girl's wan face.

" There can be nothing more to say between us now," she says, in a strange hushed voice. " Every hour you stay with me is a wrong to her. We cannot even be friends, Denzil ; for there is no medium place on which our hearts can find rest. It is very hard—very hard ! Had I known of this when I was so ill, I think I should have hardly prayed so earnestly to get well and strong. But I suppose I ought not to say this now. Oh, my dear, for the love of

Heaven leave me! I—I cannot bear this any more!"

He rises to his feet and releases her hands. A deadly struggle is at war within him, a fierce passion mingles with the sad and yearning regret for the fate he has drawn in with his own; great drops stand upon his brow; he trembles through all his strong erect frame as weakly as a woman.

"You will kiss me—once more?" he whispers, hoarsely, his whole soul going out in that last entreaty.

She cannot resist it. She forgets all, save that he was her lover — hers despite all wrongs, all ties, all barriers. She lets him draw her to his breast, and suffers him to hold her there as if no earthly power could rend her from his arms again.

"It is for the last time," she says to herself—"the last time!"

But as his lips touch hers, without moan or cry she lies there in his arms, crushed and stricken like a broken flower in a tempest.

CHAPTER V.

" YOLANDE, oh, dear Yolande! Will she never speak? "

The languid eyes unclose and rest on Enid's weeping anxious face.

" What is it? Have I been ill?" she asks, looking wonderingly around the pretty room.

" You fainted," says Enid. " Not that I wonder at it. Oh, my poor darling, I wish I could comfort you!"

Yolande sits up then. How swiftly memory comes back; and yet how calm and dead her heart feels! Presently she pushes all the bright soft hair from her forehead, and leans her head against Enid's shoulder.

" You know all?" she asks.

" Yes, dear."

" After to-day," continues the soft pained voice, " I do not want any one to speak of it again to me ; but I want to tell you, Enid, that I shall try to bear it as bravely as I can.   I am not going to make every one around me miserable out of the pure selfishness of grief ; but just at first it will not be easy, and you must bear with me— for, oh, Enid, I loved him so ! "

" I know, my darling," says the comforting voice.

" I suppose I ought not to say so now, for all is changed so utterly," goes on the sorrowful girl ; " but one cannot forget all at once.   We will go to Italy as soon as ever we can, Enid, won't we ?   I think it will be easier to think more kindly of her, less regretfully of him, when the wide sea is between us."

" We will go wherever you like, dear," says Enid, soothingly, feeling thankful that, for all its pathos, the pretty voice does not break into tears and lamentations.

"I shall still have papa to think of, and all of you to love. I wonder if it will be very hard to—not forget, I could never forget—but to think a little less of my darling who is so heart-broken now? Enid, I think it is worse for him than for me, for his hand raised the barrier between us. He can never forget that."

Enid is silent. There is a great relief in her mind that Yolande is "taking it" so much better than she anticipated ; and yet she feels a little puzzled at the strange unnatural calm in her sister's face and eyes.

"If she would cry, I could understand it," thinks Enid, distressfully.

The brave white face with its unutterable calm, the little figure sitting so still with folded hands and mute white lips, is a picture so different from the passionate grief she has expected to witness that her heart grows awed and perplexed.

"After all, I need not have been so troubled about my thinness," says Yolande, quite suddenly, the irrelevance of the words startling her sister all the more after the long pause of quiet thoughtfulness. "I don't think Denzil even noticed it!"

"Oh, Yolande," cries Enid, desperately, "don't be so cold and calm! It is all the worse for you. Do you not feel all that lies before you to bear and suffer? Oh, my dear, my dear, can you not cry as I do?"

"No," is the troubled answer. "I feel as if I had no tears to shed. My heart aches, and I know I shall be very miserable by-and-by; but I scarcely feel yet that I have lost him."

"Will you try to rest now?" says Enid, coaxingly. "Miss Llewellyn sent me up with this medicine for you. Drink it, and then try to sleep."

"Yes, I should like to sleep," returns Yolande, wistfully. "I suppose in sleep one can forget, and I was never good at dreaming, so—"

But she does not finish the sentence, though

Enid knows it just as if she had ; she drinks
the medicine—it is a sleeping draught—and
lets Enid arrange her pillows and cover her
warmly with shawls, and so lies back with
closed eyes and folded hands, utterly spent
and exhausted.

But that draught and the long, long sleep
that follows in all probability save her life
and preserve her reason.

.   .   .   .   .   .

When Denzil Charteris leaves Llewellyn
Hall it is as a crushed and heart-broken man,
a man who curses his own mad folly with
every breath he draws. There is no clear plan
of action in his mind. Yolande's words have
taken no hold of him in the bitter agony that
has held him like a spell. With the memory
of her look, with the touch of the sweet
tremulous lips growing cold, despite the passionate caress that clung to them in that
desperate farewell, there mingles only the
utter stupor of misery that even the sharpness
of despair can hardly penetrate.

She has bidden him go back to his wife; but that he knows is beyond his strength to do. Go back to her, look into her eyes, touch her hand, when, had she been a man, they would have stood face to face, with only death or bloodshed possible to avenge a wrong so vile! No, it is impossible; and yet what alternative has he?

Separation? It can bring him no nearer to his lost love. Divorce? It is impossible to obtain. The foulest treachery could not make that possible, and only of treachery can he accuse her. She will be faithful enough to him, he doubts not. It is not want of love that he can accuse her of. No—rather the reverse. But to live with her, even in common friendship—he shudders at the bare idea!

He sees her now in her true colours—vile, relentless, deceitful, not one fibre of her moral nature attuned to thought or feeling of his own. His whole soul revolts against the fearful bondage that holds him in its thrall; contact and association with the woman who bears his name and calls herself his wife seems more loathsome and abhorrent the more he thinks of it.

"It is like looking on heaven while devils hold one back!" he groans in his awful misery.

He is lying face downwards on the cushioned seat of the railway carriage, the train hurrying him swiftly back to his own most desolate home.

"Women have indeed been the curse of my life," he thinks; "this is the third time it has been marred by their hands. First, the hot wild passion of Alethea, alike unknown and undesired, that turned my brother's love to madness, and wrought his own rash end; then my own brief fancy for Pauline, which she threw over to suit her ambition; and, last, this one pure love, so real and so perfect, the love of my manhood, as fixed and as enduring as my own life, and that too is cursed by failure and disappointment."

It does indeed seem hard. All that he has

needed and found—sympathy, comprehension, love, pure yet passionate, strong and faithful as his own—all that might crown his later years with the blessings his youth has never known and vainly sought, is irretrievably lost. Do what he may, try as he may, he can see no way out of the horrible net in which his feet are entangled; and endurance seems almost beyond his strength.

The train whirls him on through the bleak, wild, desolate country; but he takes no heed of whither he goes. The trance of dull despair that holds him in its power binds all his senses in a stupor, through which only the sharp thrust of this last and worst sorrow penetrates from time to time. If anything were to happen then to end his life and his misery together, he would not care one iota. But accidents lie in wait only for the fortunate and happy; they pass by in heedless mockery, the wild despairing hearts that call to them as Denzil Charteris calls now.

" I shall either go mad, or die of longing for

sight of her sweet face!" he groans, raising
his desolate, haggard face at last. "Oh,
Heaven, my life is too hard! I have no
strength to bear it!"

The train is slackening speed now; they are
approaching a junction. He does not move,
even though he has a dim recollection of having been told he must change somewhere when
he asked for a carriage to himself. There is
much bustle and confusion and calling out of
strange Welsh names; but he only listens
mechanically to it all. How trivial appear
the common affairs of every-day life now,
when the greatness of this fresh - wrought
sorrow weighs heavily on mind and heart!

He relapses into his old position, shutting
out sense and sight alike. He never rouses
himself even when he hears the guard's voice
speaking; he fancies it is only something
about the long delay. Then, slowly at first,
but soon with increasing speed, the train
rushes on once more; and, as he raises his
face and mechanically looks round the great

dusky carriage, he sees in the corner opposite himself, but farthest removed from where he sits, the face of—his wife!

It seems to Denzil that he is the victim of some hideous dream, as he sits silently looking at the calm still figure with the triumph of revenge on her lips, the light of mockery and derision in her eyes.

One single word, hoarse as a death-cry, alone escapes his lips,—

" *You!* "

" Yes, even I," she says. " It is an unexpected pleasure to meet you here. " Have you been to Pwym Dyas?"

The mockery of her voice stings him to the quick.

He presses his hand to his heart like one suffocated by a deadly pain. The blood flushes in crimson torrents to his face. His eyes blaze with a fury that frightens this woman who has driven him to bay—and she is no coward. He springs to his feet and makes one step towards her, as, with a low, faint cry of exceeding fear, she shrinks back into the recess of the carriage.

" You may well be frightened ! " he says, in a voice wherein scorn and hatred master even the agony of blinding rage that surges within his breast. " You have done a bold thing, madam, to trust yourself in here alone with me ! Have you so little care for your life ? "

" Yes," she says, recklessly, " I have. I do not think I should care if you killed me now at this very moment. At all events, you could not wade through my blood to the little fool, who—"

" Peace ! " he thunders ; and his voice holds her silent perforce. " Dare to mention her name, and neither sex nor relationship shall save you from the vengeance of a man whose anger your mere presence turns to madness ! "

Something in his face and voice shows her in that moment all the havoc and ruin she has wrought. Involuntarily her voice softens and goes out to him in a piteous appeal.

"Denzil," she cries, "will you never forgive me? Do you not know I only erred
because I love you?"

"Love! Do not pollute the name by
applying it to the vileness and treachery
that have wrecked my whole life! Love!
Faugh! What do you know of love, when
you call your foolish revengeful frenzy, that
stooped to naught but baseness and stands
laughing in mockery of my wrongs, love?
But I waste words. Why are you here?
Are you still employing your genius as a
spy in watching my actions?"

"No," she cries, stung to fury by his
taunts; "it is accident that has brought
me hither. I do not expect you to believe
it; but I have no object in not telling you
the simple truth now."

"You do me too much honour, madam.
That means you have nothing further to gain
by lies."

"I wish I were dead!" cries the wretched
woman in a sudden paroxysm of agonised

remorse. " Oh, Denzil, I thought you might care for me in time, even a little—ever such a little ! I do not ask much, just a crumb to satisfy my starving heart, just a word that you might throw to a stranger in ordinary courtesy. I could be so patient ! You do not know ! Oh, Denzil, have you not one grain of pity for me—not one ? Even she does not—cannot love you with one half the strength and passion that are mine ! "

He looks down on her quite unmoved.

" I cannot forgive you," he said, coldly, sternly, as some inexorable fate.

" Are you so hard-hearted ? Do you think this is a mere pretence, Denzil ? Oh, believe me, it is not ! All my chance of becoming a better woman lies in your hands. If you send me from you, I shall grow desperate. Don't have my blood on your hands, my sins on your soul, as you have the blood of another of your fated race ! Denzil—husband, it is my last appeal ! Oh, for the love of Heaven, hear me ! I will never ask you again after to-day!"

"Did you heed me," he says, "when I cried to you—when you stole to my side in my madness and despair, and, knowing who had dealt this deadly wrong, yet denied to me as well as to yourself all power of reparation ? No, it is beyond my strength; I cannot grant your prayer!"

"Then, as Heaven hears me, I will end my life!" she cries, wildly. "On your head be my blood, Denzil Charteris!" And, ere he can stay her or fathom her intention, she has flung open the carriage door, and sprung upon the step.

He sees the desperate face, the mad action; he hears the wild cry. Then—how, he knows not—his arm is round her. With one hand he clutches the swaying door, with the other he holds her, struggling, quivering, panting like a wounded deer. She cannot release herself from his grasp, try as she may. The cold keen air blows fiercely, swiftly by; the trees and telegraph-posts race on in mad confusion. Then, swift as a lightning-flash that rends a cloud, comes a shock—a crash. The panting engine seems to rear like a living, furious thing ; and, amid fire and smoke and hissing steam, Denzil is conscious only of a falling blow that lays him prostrate on the carriage floor, deaf and insensible to all that follows.

CHAPTER VI.

OLSTON is a quiet, sleepy, though by no means small town, with nothing to boast of in the shape of architectural beauty. It has a market-place and a bank, a theatre and a town-hall, a few good streets, an immense number of bad ones, a great many churches, one or two chapels, a railway station, and some of the dingiest, purlieus imaginable leading from the outskirts of the town into the country lanes and roads, which in their turn stretch away to pretty picturesque Ashbourne.

In one of the dingiest and narrowest and worst-famed of these streets stands a little public-house bearing the sign of "The Spotted Dog." Such a miserable dwelling it is, and

bearing so little appearance of anything likely
to tempt customers, that the notices of " Good
beds " and " Pea soup and sausages, sixpence "
are seemingly looking out of the opaque
window-panes in irony, or put up as baits to
trap the unwary. Certainly rest and refreshment look far enough away from the unsavoury
obscure place.

One dark winter night, however, a customer
does look in at that humble tavern and boldly
orders a steak and pint of ale as refreshment.
The fat landlord lounging in the bar looks
curiously at the newcomer, and growls out a
summons to his slipshod, slovenly wife to
attend to his wants. The stranger meanwhile
seats himself at one of the tables covered
with sticky oilcloth, and bearing innumerable
impressions of the wet bottoms of pewter
pots and prepares to wait with commendable
patience for the arrival of his supper. The
fat landlord, having apparently overcome his
momentary distrust, lounges in from the bar
and stirs the dreary fire into a blaze, and

makes an apologetic attempt to wipe the sticky table with his not over-clean apron.

" Bad night this," he says by way of conversation.

" True enough," answers the other.

" Are you a stranger to these parts ? " demands the landlord, presently.

" Yes. I came as gardener to Mr Herrick the lawyer a month or so ago," is the frank rejoinder.

" Oh, ay ! A close-fisted tough old customer your master, bean't he ? "

" It ain't much concern of mine," answers the younger man. " He pays my wages, and that's all I care about. His place is dreary enough, but I manage to give 'em the slip now and then, and make off for Colston when I want a spree."

" You don't go to Ashbourne ? " queries the landlord.

" Sometimes ; but it's not so much in my line. 'Tis a dull place at best."

" How came you to find out this place ? "

asks the man, with a suspicious glance at the smooth inscrutable face beside him. " Strangers as a rule are not over-quick at finding their way to the worst part o' the town. We've some rough customers here sometimes, I can tell you; and a dandy chap like you wouldn't be over and above safe if they didn't happen to be in a humour to see you."

" Oh, I'm not afraid!" returns the other. " A public's a public, I suppose ? I lost my way in looking out for some confounded seed-shop that I had to. go to; that's how I came here. I sha'n't interfere with any of yer customers, I lay."

" Are you a Londoner ?" demands his host.

" No ; I come from Doncaster ; but I've been in London a goodish bit."

" I wonder you don't stop there then ; this part of the country is hardly the sort for men o' your mettle."

The man shrugs his shoulders.

" One can't always pick and choose," he

says. "I'd been out of work a long time, and was getting hard up when I heard of Mr Herrick. It's a dull enough place ; but it'll do for me a while."

"You smoke maybe ?" questions the landlord, taking out a short dirty clay, and proceeding to light it.

"Oh, yes," answers the other, cheerfully ; "and, if you think my supper's going to be much longer, I'll join you with pleasure. Shall I order some beer ? Smoking's dry work."

The host evinces no objection to this suggestion, and even retires to draw a jug of some special brew which his customer shrewdly suspects is from a private tap reserved for himself.

Then they draw the table nearer to the fire, and sit down to discuss their pipes and exchange opinions on matters in general. The landlord, in thinking about this evening afterwards, finds it difficult to account for the manner in which the conversation turned to the murder in Dead Man's Pool—a topic stale enough to his mind and possessing little interest.

"There be a letter in to-day's *Advertiser* 'bout that very thing," he says, presently, his tongue wagging freer after the copious libations of strong ale he has swallowed at his customer's expense. "It gives it sharp to local police and local juries, that it do, and as good as hints that once they had the real culprit pretty nigh at hand, and yet let him slip through their fingers."

"Oh," observes the young man, thoughtfully, "it seems a queer 'fair, don't it? I suppose it would never have been found out if that gentleman from the Proiry hadn't disappeared?"

"No, that it wouldn't," says the man, "and yet— But there—it's no good a-tellin' suspicions now. I don't want any of those darned peelers a pokin' and pryin' into my concerns. When they find the murderer, it's time enough to speak about the feller as was murdered."

"Then you know something of him," asserts the stranger, quietly.

The man takes his black pipe out of his mouth and bends a little nearer.

"I don't mind tellin' you, as you be a stranger here," he says, in a thick uncertain voice—the effect probably of deep potations—"I don't mind tellin' you, young man, that I've a strong suspicion in my mind as how I knows that 'ere chap whom no one could 'dentify—isn't that what they call it?"

"Yes," answers the stranger, with suppressed eagerness, though he fills the bowl of his pipe quite calmly even as he speaks. "Now you do surprise me!"

"Yes; I know a thing or two more than people quite give me credit for," continues the old Silenus, helping himself to another glass, as his companion pushes the jug towards him.

"I should fancy you did," returns his companion, with judicious flattery. "But you were saying—"

"Here's your supper, I do believe," says the

host, turning his bleared eyes towards the door. "No—not yet. I'll give that old woman a rousing—by Jove, I will, if she don't look a bit sharper after a customer than what she's doing to-night! Half a mortal hour ha' you been sitting here, waiting for that bit o' steak!"

"Never mind," says the young man, soothingly—"I'm not very hungry. Perhaps your wife was busy."

"Busy!" growls the old man. "She ha'n't got no call to be busy; she's only the lodger's supper and your's. Yes, that's my lodger sitting down there—old Job we call him. A rum old cove he is. You needn't take any notice of him; he's always like that."

The under-gardener's sharp grey eyes are fixed carelessly but yet intently upon the strange shambling figure that has entered the parlour. It is the bent, almost humpbacked figure of an old man—a man with white hair in straggling elf-locks about his shoulders, and a pair of blue spectacles fixed over his eyes.

He has a curious habit of always rubbing his hands softly together, and apparently talking to himself in a semi-whisper, utterly regardless of any observers. After one long curious glance the young man turns to his host again, but further conversation is for a time interrupted by the entrance of the landlady with the long-delayed supper, and the interchange of a few little social amenities between herself and her liege lord, whom she designates as a " boosing old sot," a remark, the far from complimentary nature of which, seems to ruffle his temper exceedingly.

The steak is very tough and unappetising, and the customer does not appear to possess much appetite. He orders, however, some hot rum-and-water, at which the landlord's eyes sparkle with rapture, and of which he shows even greater willingness to partake, than he has before displayed for the ale.

Were he at all suspicious now, he might wonder that the young man presses the drinks so hard upon him, and partakes so sparingly of

them himself ; but his soddened brain is beyond all such power of reasoning ; and he lets
his skilful questioner get out of him the story
he has already begun, without offering any
objection to his skilful cross-questioning or
suspecting that any sinister motive lurks
beneath the seemingly careless interest.

" It were a matter of some nine or ten
months ago "—so he begins his narrative—
" when a queer foreign-looking, foreign-spoken
chap looked in here—as it might be you looking in to-night—and ' Can I have a lodging ? '
says he. I told him ' Yes,' he could, and he
ordered his supper and took a look at his
room and said it would do. He had no lug-
gage of any sort, and was dressed very quiet-
like—just as any gentleman might be dressed
—and he sat there, just as it might be where
old Job is sitting now "—the young man
glances at the lodger, and sees him peering
eagerly through his blue spectacles at the
greasy torn paper which the landlord has
been reading—" yes, just where old Job is

sitting now," reiterates the narrator, and his hearer fancies that there is a strange quiver in the newspaper that the quiet reader holds, but then he tells himself, " Old men's hands are apt to tremble." " He spoke little," continues the landlord, " and the room was pretty full of men, all smoking and drinking and talking away together. Presently this stranger comes up to me, ' Landlord,' he says, ' do you know where Inspector Budd, of Colston, lives ? ' "

As the narrator again pauses to partake of some of the rum-and-water the eyes of the quiet listener again turn to the figure opposite. As his glance darts forward, the newspaper is cautiously moved aside, and for one second he catches sight of the blue spectacles, not resting over the eyes now, but pushed up on the forehead.

" Humph ! " says the young gardener to himself. " That man's disguised as sure as I live ! Is this some one else on the scent with an eye to the reward, or—" But the last suggestion hold him breathless. He dares not trust himself to follow it up. "Go on," he says, to the host, who is evincing far greater interest in his grog than in his narrative.

" There's not much more to tell," returns the landlord huskily. "I said I knew the inspector very well — which was true. I knowed him a deal better than I wanted. He said could he have a message sent to him perticular that night? I said ' Yes,' if he liked to pay for it. He laughed, and said he'd more money than 'ud keep twenty such publics as this! I said, ' Don't brag too loud, for there's a rough set of customers here.' Well, to make it short, I sent the message, and the boy brought an answer back. It was written on a scrap of paper ; and he swore and cursed in fine lingo when he read it. He went to bed, and the next morning he asked the way to Beechhampton Woods, and I directed him as well as I could. He paid his bill, and told me he shouldn't be back in these parts again.

He gave me a five-pound note and said he wanted no change. Sez I, ' You seem to have a rum lot of money about you.' ' Yes,' he says, ' and it's nearly all in paper ; and every one of these bank-notes is marked like that one I've given you.' Well, I was never much of a scholar ; so I asked him what that mark was. ' It's M-a-y,' he says, ' the name of my sweetheart. She were the prettiest lass in Suffolk, and we were to be wed as soon as I came back from sea ; but I was wrecked, and then kept in a foreign prison, and no one knew anything of me for many a long year ; and when I went to look for her I heard she'd gone away wi' another chap—a mean sneak as I'd always hated ever since we were boys at the old national school together. I didn't believe it when I heard of it ; but I shall know soon whether it's true or not.' I won-dered a little at his saying that ; but I thought no more of it. He went away towards Beech-hampton, whistling quite cool and calmly. I never see'd him again."

" But he said he was not coming back, didn't he ? " inquires the attentive listener.

" Yes ; and I shouldn't have thought so much of that," returns the landlord, leaning forward and speaking in an awed and troubled voice, " only, look you here—"

But ere he can speak the words he wishes, the door is burst riotously open, and three ill-dressed, savage-looking men enter, calling vociferously for jugs of porter and ale, and indulging in much coarse bantering of old Job, which he neither answers nor seems to hear.

The fat landlord leaves his snug nook by the fire to attend to his customers' wants, and the gardener sits there alone, fidgeting impatiently for his host's return, which seems likely to be long protracted.

The silent old man still sits with the news-paper before him, apparently quite unmoved by the noise around. The blue spectacles are replaced, and even the searching eyes bent upon him can see nothing but a shabby, decrepit-looking old man, following with a dirty trembling finger the lines of the news spread out before him.

" He's not quite wrinkled and leathery enough for that white hair," thinks the sharp-eyed watcher. "I should like to know what his little game is ! "

Presently the individual in question puts down the newspaper, takes up his hat, and shuffles off without a word to anybody.

" That's his way always," says the landlord, coming over to his first customer and handing him his bill, in accordance with his request. " Queer ? Well, I daresay it is ; but we're used to it now."

" Has he been with you long ? " inquires the gardener, handing a sovereign, after having run his eye over the items of the bill.

" Two—no, three weeks," answers the man.

"And what does he do—generally speaking?"

" Plods about, and gets odd jobs about the town, so he says. I don't know. I never watches my lodgers. 'Twouldn't pay."

"I suppose not," says the younger man, thoughtfully. "Well, I must be going homewards now," he adds, as the clock strikes ten.

"Ay ; I should think you're an uncommon free and easy chap to go stopping out like this !" answers his host, coming out with him into the bar. "I al'ays thought Squire Herrick shut up every hole and corner of his rabbit-warren yonder at ten every night."

"No, half-past," corrects the man, lighting his pipe as he speaks. "A bad night, isn't it, for a long tramp ? "

"Ay, ay!" returns the landlord, gruffly. "You know your way though, I suppose ? "

"Oh, yes !" answers the other, cheerfully. "I know it right enough." Then, as if by some impulse, he lays his hand on the landlord's arm. "You broke off your story just at the most interesting part," he says, persuasively. "Won't you tell me what you were going to say ? "

For a moment the man hesitates and looks around suspiciously.

"I don't know as how I ought to say anything about it," he says, slowly at last.
"Howsomever, I don't suppose you'll be getting me into trouble about it. You're one of
the silent sort, I'm thinking, though you are
free and open enough with your money. Well,
what I was going to say was this. Last
market-day, when I went to the Corn Exchange, I got a note given me in payment
of summat a chap there owed me. I don't
care particular for notes, and I was handing
it back, asking him to give me gold instead,
when my eye fell on the back of it. It made
me feel downright queer for a minute, for
there, staring me in the face, just as I was
giving it to the chap, was the same mark
as was on my own note at home—M-a-y."

"Had you not changed your note, then?"
asks the man, with suppressed eagerness.

"No; I've got it still."

"But the man you spoke of might have
changed others of his notes in the town beside
the one he gave you," suggests the gardener.

"He might—true," says the landlord, huffily ; "but I don't believe he ever did— even if he had the chance !" And, without another word, he waddles back into the bar, slamming the outer door, and shutting out his customer with the blackness and dark- ness of the stormy winter night.

CHAPTER VII.

FTER that evening, in the course of which the landlord of " The Spotted Dog " had been so communicative, it is a noteworthy fact that Mr Herrick's under-gardener is a very frequent visitor to that place of entertainment.

Twice or thrice at least in every week does he make his appearance, flinging his coins recklessly into the landlord's till, standing treat to him and many of his colleagues with munificent generosity, and winning the character of being "a rare free-handed chap, with no nonsense about him." On these evenings, old Job never deviates from his course of action. At the same hour he always comes in, orders his frugal supper, drinks his pint of ale, reads the paper while the others talk, jest, and swear in their various fashions, and then takes himself off to bed without word or warning. At the gardener's third visit he endeavours to make overtures to old Job of a similar nature to those by which he has earned the goodwill of the rough customers who usually frequent the public-house ; but his advances meet with no encouragement ; and, though old Job drinks willingly enough at his expense, his potations only make him surlier, denser, and more impenetrable than ever. Still Dowling perseveres in his efforts with remarkable good nature. In the object he has in view patience is the surest weapon for conquering all difficulties ; and the greasy note-book carried in the under-gardener's breast-pocket bears many a memorandum of these apparently wasted evenings, that would have greatly astonished his colleagues.

There is plenty of vagabondage going on around, and mysterious meetings and collo-

quies often take place between suspicious-
looking individuals who drop in to drink and
smoke and talk thieves' jargon in corners, or
make bets on horses, or discuss the Derby and
the forthcoming Leger and the Cup, and quarrel
and swear and behave generally in a manner
utterly at variance with the tenets of decent
society. But Dowling pays no heed to these
individuals, though he makes many a private
note of their names and aliases; and they
grow so accustomed to the sight of the quiet
good-humoured-looking stranger, who so freely
treats them to liquors and looks so super-
latively unconscious of their jargon, that the
distrust with which they had at first received
him completely vanishes.

"Have you heard the folks are back at
Beechhampton?" he says, one evening, as he
sits puffing clouds of bird's-eye, and keeping
one eye, as usual, on the bent and withered-
looking figure of old Job.

"Ay," answers the landlord. "A fat lot
of good that Mr Charteris do do here. He's

no sooner back at the Priory than he's off again."

"He had a nearish shave of his life in that railway accident a while ago, hadn't he?" pursues Dowling.

"Yes; they do say as madam won't ever recover. Her spine's injured, or summat o' that sort. He had only a broken arm."

"Where have they been all this time, do you suppose?" questions the other.

"Down at the little Welsh place close to where the accident was," is the reply. "Leastways the papers says so—don't they, Job?"

"Iss," grunts that worthy from behind the sheets of the local journal he is perusing.

"Well, he don't appear going to have much comfort out of his married life," continues the landlord. "It was a queer affair, so suddint and secret-like; and then he getting ill, and when he were only fit for bed—so the servants said—a-startin' off to goodness knows where, and she and he being in the Welsh train as

was going back to the very place he had left.
They say he should have changed to the down
express and didn't. But she were mortal injured—and he's pretty well damaged too, I'm
thinking."

Mrs Charteris is very beautiful, is she not ?"
inquires Dowling.

" I dunno," returns the man, surlily. " She
be a fine dashing woman, but not one as I'd
like to know. Was you speaking, Job ? "

A grunt was the only reply.

" I've not seen her," says the gardener,
thoughtfully.

" And I don't s'pose you will now, if what
the paper says be true," answers the landlord.
" She won't be able to move off her couch again."

" Serve her right too ! "

The furious tone in 'which these words are
uttered makes Dowling and his host stare in
unqualified amazement at the speaker.

" Why Job," exclaims the latter, " what are
you a-talkin' of ? How do you know aught of
Mrs Charteris ? Have you ever seen her ? "

But the old man only grunts some unintelligible remark, and relapses into impenetrable silence once more.

"Will you have some pine-apple rum, Job?" asks Dowling, presently. "It'll warm yer old bones. This is an awful cold night and no mistake."

The old man lays down his paper and shambles along towards the chimney-corner. It is his usual method of accepting an invitation ; he never wastes words on anybody.

The steaming glass of rum-and-water seems in no way to thaw his icy gloom and impenetrability ; but Dowling and his host go on with their pipes and conversation, bestowing very little notice on the shabby, dreary old figure bending and shivering over the fire.

"So your theatre's going to open next week?" remarks Dowling, presently.

"Ay," grunts the landlord.

"Does it ever pay?" inquires the gardener.

"Dunno. Never go a-wasting my money on such trash," is the grim rejoinder.

"Wal, now, I like the theatre," says the younger man. "It does one good to see a rale fine bit of playacting now and then. When I lived at Doncaster I went continual."

"There's another queer set out, a-coming on at the Town Hall," adds the host, taking a deep draught of his fragrant beverage. "A magician, or wizard, or something he calls himself. He does a power of wonderful things—makes people go to sleep and tell him all he wants them to tell, and sends watches through hats, and rings through handkerchiefs, and goldfishes come into a bowl of water, and I dunno what all."

"Indeed!" says the younger man, thoughtfully, "that must be nigh as good as the theatre. Have you got it there in the paper?"

"Yes," answers the other, stretching out his hand for the greasy well-thumbed journal, and handing it to Dowling.

The latter looks carelessly at the ostentatious advertisements of the wonderful and renowned Wizard of the West, who will give

his marvellous entertainment, comprising mes-
merism, ventriloquism, magic, and legerdemain,
at the Town Hall, Colston, for three nights
only.

Then follows a description of the allitera-
tive advertiser's feats and accomplishments,
which Dowling peruses with a smile of in-
credulity. He turns next to the theatre,
and reads the programme of that fascinating
abode which is rarely open more than
three months in the year, and has been the
ruin of many an enterprising manager and
starring company.

" *The Bells,*" he says ; " I never heard or
saw that before. A queer enough name,
isn't it ? "

" As good as any other," grunts the landlord. " I've heard of it somewhere ; it made
a bit of a hit at Manchester—I think it was
Manchester. A customer of mine were talking
about it. He says, says he, ' I never felt so
downright queer as when I saw that piece.
'Tis all about a murder done by some foreign

chap—a mayor, or something of the sort—
and no one knows or guesses it all his life.
He must have been a rare, artful cove
that!'"

A crash of glass interrupts the speaker
and startles Dowling.

"Job, you mortal old stupid!" cries the
irate landlord. "There, if you haven't been
and smashed your glass. My missus'll be
fine and rampageous with you, I know."

"I—I'll buy another!" says old Job, trying to gather up the broken fragments with
his trembling fingers.

"Won't you have another glass?" asks
Dowling, cheerily. "You didn't drink half
your rum!"

"No more, no more!" cries the old man,
huskily, as he shuffles off in his usual un-
ceremonious fashion. "Don't be angry,
Harris, don't be angry! I'll buy you another glass—oh, yes, I'll buy you another
glass!"

"Queer old cuss that!" remarks Dowling

as the door closes. "Nerves seem shaky, don't you think ?"

"Something seems shaky about him to-night," answers the other, gruffly. "It isn't often he trembles like that, old as he is."

"Well, I must be going now," says the young man, rising and pushing back his chair. "You don't care for the theatre, Harris, you say, or else I'd treat you. I mean to go and see *The Bells* the first night it is performed."

"Seems to me your master allows you a jolly sight more liberty than you ought to have," returns the other.

"As long as I do my work, no one has any call to interfere with me," retorts Dowling; "and, if I have the bad taste to prefer your public to a heap of other better and cleaner ones in the town, you oughtn't to complain, I'm sure."

"Who's complaining?" growls Harris, sur-lily. "I'm glad enough to see you when you

comes in for your drop o' grog and your pipe.
I can't say more, can I ? "

" No," laughs Dowling, heartily—"and I
don't want you to. But about the theatre ? "

" Hang the theatre ! " exclaims the other.
" I'm not goin' to any theatres; so don't waste
your time asking me."

" All right. Then I shall go alone. I've
got a fancy to see the piece ! "

.   .   .   .   .   .

The Theatre Royal, Colston, like most other
theatres in country towns, is small, dingy,
ill-built, and badly ventilated. On the night
on which the opening performance of the
starring company is given it is tolerably well
filled. The piece is new to the general public;
and the principal actor, who, since its produc-
tion in the provinces, has made for himself a
wide-spread and universal fame, is here also.

Mr James Dowling betakes himself to the
pit, and, after a rapid survey of the house,
makes himself as comfortable as circumstances
permit, the said circumstances being repre-

sented by squalling babies, pushing children,
noisy women and half-tipsy men. The performance begins very punctually with a farce,
in which there is a good deal of cellar-and-
cupboard business, and a young man in alarm-
ing check trousers is constantly occupied in
hiding himself from the discovery of an irate
parent. Mr James Dowling is apparently not
very hard to please, for he laughs heartily,
applauds immensely, and behaves as one of
the approved patrons of the British drama
generally does behave.

When the curtain draws up for the great
piece of the evening, however, his face grows
grave and watchful. As the first act proceeds it grows rather perplexed ; and, when
the curtain falls, he applauds merely mechanically.

"I'm hanged if I can make it out!" he
mutters, rising and giving himself a shake, as
if to waken his brain from its bewilderment.
Standing thus, he suddenly faces round, and
with a rapid lightning-like glance sweeps the

gallery above him. His quiet face flushes
ever so slightly, a smile of ill-concealed
triumph quivers round the firm compressed
lips. " I thought so," he says to himself,
turning away his eyes, and letting his face
resume its expression of habitual indifference.
" By Jove ! I do believe I'm getting on the
scent at last !"

The curtain rises again ; the play goes on.
The betrothal of the Burgomaster's daughter
to Christian, the signing of the marriage con-
tract, the strange and marvellously-conquered
agitation of the man, who, at the very moment
of the fulfilment of his dearest hopes, hears
the haunting, ill-omened sound of the sleigh-
bells of his victim—all these pass before the
young man's eyes, yet scarcely impress him as
he had expected to be impressed. A thrill of
disappointment runs through him as the
curtain falls once more to applause that is
very faint and weak.

" I didn't see much in it after all," he
thinks.

And then his mind reverts to the momentary glimpse of the haggard face and white straggling locks of the man in the gallery, the man who had shrunk back with down-bent head into his seat as the glance of those sharp piercing eyes detected him.

The opening of the third act rouses him from his meditative trance. Once more he turns his eyes upon the stage, carelessly, wearily enough ; then— Ah ! what is it that rouses his wandering attention and holds him silent, spell-bound by the weird and mystic scene ? The stage grows dark and dim, yet from the darkness looms, faint and indistinct, a shadowy circle of figures. The piercing eyes soon make them out to be a court of justice. With all the mystic meaning of a dream, that strange weird scene goes on. The stern voice of the judge rings out, the defiant answer of the accused comes firm and hard in answer. Piece after piece of evidence is confuted, until at last there issues forth the strange command,—

" Bring hither the mesmerist ! "

The wild hoarse cry that follows from the lips of the haunted, despairing man seems to curdle the very blood in the veins of the awe-struck, breathless audience. Not a sound is heard now ; every eye is fixed, every ear strained as the awful spectacle proceeds, where science forces the guilty soul to act out its own red-handed drama, to shadow forth with deadly certainty each action of a deed of blood.

James Dowling's face looks like an iron mask in its cold, rigid horror. He scarce draws breath, he moves neither eye nor limb until the scene fades like the dream it has represented ; and on the lighted stage are confused figures and frightened faces grouped around the guilty man, who dies in the horror of that awful dream, that to the spectators seems no dream at all.

Blind, confused, his usual steady brain in a whirl, his usual firm step shaking and trem-bling like a drunkard's, the detective rushes forth from the wild weird scene into the cold and stormy darkness without.

"I have it now!" he cries to himself in riotous triumph. "Ere a week is over my head my task will be ended, as sure as my name is—not James Dowling!"

CHAPTER VIII.

"YOU must be mad, Dowling!" says Mr Herrick the next morning, as he paces up and down the garden with the new gardener. "I never heard of such a preposterous suggestion!"

"All's fair in war and—justice, sir," returns the man, with a queer twinkle in his eye. "If you'll only give your consent to the experiment, I'll be bound to have the case all cut and dry before you for the next assizes."

"What makes you so confident?" asks the lawyer.

"I can't tell you, sir ; only I'm pretty sure I've scented my man out at last. My only fear is he'll give us the slip if we don't look sharp. I notice he's a deal too fond of looking at the shipping-lists lately. Come, sir, haven't you got confidence enough in me to trust me in this instance? I only want your consent and a promise of a fiver to that rum old cove who calls himself the Wizard—as nice an old party to speak to as ever I met, he is too, though he dresses himself a bit outlandish."

"Well, I don't know what to think of it," says Mr Herrick, in a puzzled tone. "It's the queerest suggestion I ever heard of in all my life! I don't know that it's quite fair either to the man."

"Anything's fair to such a wily old dodger as that," replies Mr Dowling, contemptuously. "It's my belief he's living on the money got from that poor murdered chap all this time. I've traced two of those marked notes back to him."

"Ay, that was very clever of you," says the old lawyer, approvingly; "but I want to know how you're going to prove old Job, as you call him, to be our friend that we're look-ing after. You can't tell him—he's disguised;

and, 'pon my honour, Dowling, the man you pointed out to me the day we tracked the old man is as different as possible from—Budd."

" Hush ! "—and the detective looks cautiously round. "Not so loud, please, sir. No one must get wind of our being on the lookout for that gentleman, if you ever mean us to catch him."

" But why should he be living here so close to the place—in the very neighbourhood where he might be most easily recognised ? " exclaims the old lawyer, impatiently.

" Ay, why ? " returns Dowling, softly. " Why do murderers always do just the one silly, soft thing that leads to discovery ? That's the puzzle, sir ! They're so mighty clever that some little foolish every-day circumstance, of which they never think, convicts them. But it's a law of Providence, I think, that, sooner or later, they must come back to the place of their crime. They don't seem as if they could help it. I suppose they think no one's likely to look for them there. But, to return to our 'mutton,' Mr Herrick, will you give in to me in this? I can't get a warrant out on the very slight suspicions I have formed; they're strong enough to me, but two people rarely look at things with the same eyes. A bold stroke may carry the game, hesitation may lose it. Which is it to be?"

"Well, you must have your way, I suppose," says the old lawyer, after a lengthy pause. "Manage it the best way you can; though how you mean to get over that scoundrelly old Harris puzzles me; also how you suppose Job, or whatever he calls himself, is going to be foolish enough to submit to such an operation!"

"Bless your heart, sir, he won't know a word of it!" chuckles the detective. "Trust me and the Wizard for that! As for Harris, he's got his price, like most people, and I'll give him a pretty strong hint as to what he'd better do in the matter. All I want you to do, sir, is to remain out of sight till I give the signal. Then you can come in and put the old chap up to what he's to ask."

" It's the most extraordinary idea—really the most extraordinary idea I ever heard of ! " says Mr Herrick, in an odd, bewildered tone.

" Well, you see, sir, we live in extraordinary days," answers the detective, with a faint quiver of amusement round his grave mouth. " And why shouldn't science be brought to bear on criminal cases as well as on other things ? I don't see it, I'm sure."

" It will be a wrinkle for law-courts and the private police, I must say," says Mr Herrick, grimly.

" There's no occasion for any of them to hear of it," answers Mr Dowling. " You see, sir, it's quite private-like. If my idea's right, we accuse him boldly ; if not, there's no harm done, and old Job is old Job still—not a farthing's worth the wiser for all he's been saying and doing. I got it all out of the old cove myself ; there's no risk, no fear— nothing. He'll just go off to sleep like a

lamb; you ask all your questions through
the mesmerist, and there you are!"

"There I am indeed!" says Mr Herrick.
"It's a bold stroke, and no mistake, Dowling. I only hope it's all right."

"Right as a trivet, sir! You trust me,"
is the confident answer. "Now I'm just
going to rake up those 'ere beds, and this
afternoon I go to Colston for those seeds as
you want so particular, and which haven't
come. And to-night—"

"To-night indeed!" says Mr Herrick,
gravely. "I wish it may be all as well as
you imagine, Dowling."

.   .   .   .   .   .

It is close upon nine o'clock, and the parlour of "The Spotted Dog" looks even more
gloomy and disreputable than usual. The
fat landlord sits near the fire, imbibing pine-
apple rum; but his usual surly countenance
bears an expression of intense fear, and his
restless glances wander incessantly from James
Dowling's face to the slipshod figure of old

Job, who sits in his usual corner poring over the newspaper.

" Have some rum, Job ? " inquires Dowling, presently. " What an unsociable chap you are ! Come, put down that paper and join us. We're dull enough to-night as it is. What's become of all your customers, Harris ? "

" Dunno," growls that worthy.

" I don't mind if I do have a glass to-night," says old Job, with unwonted loquacity. " I shall be a-goin' off from here to-morrow, Harris. I've heerd of a job as'll likely suit me, and I'm going to see after it."

" Oh, indeed ! " says Dowling, leaning back in his chair and yawning lazily. " And are you going far ? "

" That be my business," is the curt rejoinder.

" True for you," says Dowling, bending down to strike a match on the heel of his boot. " Well, here's good luck to you ! "

They drain their glasses, and, as they put them down, the door opens and a stranger comes in. He is a tall, thin man, very shabby and poverty-stricken in appearance, with a pale, strange face and dark sombre eyes. The landlord rises to greet him and to supply his wants. Dowling and Job, after a careless glance, go on with their employment of mixing fresh tumblers of rum-and-water. Old Job is opportunely in a sociable mood, and actually condescends to answer Dowling's remarks, and give that astute individual a surly account of his forthcoming change of location, and the duties he has undertaken— all of which his hearer knows to be utterly false. Presently, however, the old man seems to grow uncomfortable. He twists and turns about in his chair, his words come in a short, jerky fashion, and his eyes wander restlessly about the room.

Dowling apparently pays no attention to these symptoms. Presently, to his great surprise, the old man rises and crosses over to where the pale, odd-looking stranger is sitting.

The new arrival takes no notice of him, beyond raising his eyes and giving a sharp, rapid glance at his face.

Then he says, in a low soft voice,—

"Remove your spectacles."

Without a word or sign of remonstrance the old man obeys.

"Sit down," continues the stranger.

With a deep sigh old Job sinks into a chair, his eyes still resting in absorbed, yet reluctant intentness, on those strange sombre orbs that are fixed on him.

Dowling lays down his pipe and watches the two in breathless silence. The stranger stands up now and makes a few rapid passes over the man's head. Then he turns to the detective.

"He's off now," he says, quietly. "He's a wonderfully easy subject; he only resisted for half a minute."

"Are you quite sure he's not shamming?" asks Dowling, approaching and gazing awestruck at the trance-sleeper.

" Sure ? " exclaims the stranger, scornfully.
" I wish I was as sure of having a thousand
pounds this minute."

" Shall I call in the others ? " asks Dowling,
respectfully.

" Certainly. Have you any questions you
wish me to ask him ? "

" Not yet ; the other gentleman is to do
that," says Dowling, going to the door.

A moment later Mr Herrick and the landlord enter together. The lawyer gives a keen,
critical glance at the calm sleeping figure, and
then turns to the host.

" Be good enough to lock your door," he
says. " I daresay you know me ; I'm Mr
Herrick, the lawyer. I've reason to suspect this
man of an ill deed, and I call upon you to bear
witness to anything that may occur to-night."

" I don't want to stand in the way of
justice, squire," returns the man in his usual
surly tone, "but I don't know what you're a
hocussin' of that poor old chap for ; it don't
seem fair play to me, that it don't."

"You hold your tongue and drink your grog ; that's all you've got to do, my friend," says Mr Dowling, approaching. "I'm John Clarke, of Scotland Yard. You've heard of me before to-day, or I'm much mistaken."

The discomfited Harris, to whom that well-known name is a signal-word of terror, collapses immediately at this remark, and, with no attempt at reply, seats himself by his favourite chimney-corner to watch the proceedings.

To all appearance, the suspected man is quietly asleep. His colour is as fresh, his breathing as regular, as a child's.

"Your questions, sir," says the mesmerist, turning to Mr Herrick.

"Ask him whether he is disguised or not," is the quiet answer.

"Yes," is the response of the man ; and, expected though it is, neither the lawyer nor the detective can repress a slight start of surprise at the ready affirmation.

"For what reason ?" is the next question.

"To avoid detection," comes from the unconscious lips that are sealing the doomed man's fate.

" Why do you wish to avoid detection ? "

There is a strong shuddering sigh. It seems as if the bound and controlled spirit seeks to resist the indomitable will that forces it to respond ; but in vain—in vain.

" Because—*I am a guilty man.*"

The grim old lawyer's face grows paler than usual ; the detective's mask of impenetrability is lighted by a gleam of triumph in his calm grey eyes. But neither of them speaks. In the chimney-corner sits the landlord, his pipe and glass alike forgotten as his wondering gaze takes in that strange group.

" Ask him," says Mr Herrick, presently, " to describe what took place on the evening of the 20th of January last."

" I had a note from Gabriel Lorton, a man I had not seen for half a score of years ; I thought he was dead. I had done him a great wrong once, and had no wish to see him again. He found me out on his return from sea and

tracked me here," comes slowly and mono-
tonously from the sleeper's lips.

" What did the note say ? "

" He asked me to meet him."

" Did you consent ? "

" I wrote and bade him be in the Beechhampton Woods, at a spot I described, the next
afternoon."

" What followed ? "

For a moment there is a hesitating silence.
The face of the man grows convulsed, his body
writhes as from some strange inward torture ;
but a wave of the mesmerist's hand stops the
paroxysm, and his breathing grows calm ; it is
the last struggle of the weaker will against
the stronger.

His head drops on his breast.   The inexorable voice goes on,—

" What followed ?   Tell me all."

" I met him at the entrance to the woods.
I led him on to the most sequestered part.
He insisted upon knowing what had become
of the girl to whom he had been betrothed

when he sailed for that foreign port. We
had been rivals once, and he hated me as I
hated him. He said he had found out she
had left the village where she lived until then.
Where was she now? I told him she had
loved me better than him—that I had wedded
her, and we had been happy together for
many years—then she died. As I told him
that, he flew at me like a tiger. He said that
I was a lying hound, that I had killed her. I
knew he was right. I knew that the girl had
broken her heart for love of him—had pined
away like a dying flower from the moment she
had become my wife. His words maddened
me; my blood was up. I had hated him
always. I had hated him more since the
only woman I ever loved had left me alone
and burdened with misery. I have always
been reckoned a soft, good-natured, easy-going
man; but no one ever knew what a demon
lurked in the depths of my heart, ready to
spring up at the provocation of such a
moment. He was a strong man; but the

strength of a hundred fiends was raging in me. When his hand touched my throat I grew mad. The air seemed filled with voices shrieking, 'Kill him, kill him!' A sea of blood seemed to float before my eyes. We wrestled together silently. I think he must have seen there was murder in my look, he grew so pale; yet no word escaped him—no prayer for mercy. My hands pressed tighter and closer on his throat. He was like a child in my grasp. I saw the veins swell, the starting eyes, and heard the suffocating gasp; then his strength failed, his arms relaxed—he fell at my feet like a log—dead!"

A shudder of horror runs through the listening men; only the pale face of the mesmerist remains unchanged.

"Go on," the calm, icy voice commands.

"I was stunned for a moment. I knelt there and tried to revive him. It was useless; he was quite dead. I searched his pockets then; I dared not let anything remain about him by which he could be identified. I found nothing but a silk hand-kerchief, a pocket-book full of bank notes, and a few loose coins. I took them all, then dragged the body to a place I knew of, where there was no likelihood of any living being ever approaching, and dropped it in the deep stagnant waters of a pool. Then I went home."

" When the body was found, long after-wards, why did you try to persuade every one it was the corpse of Mr Charteris of Beechhampton ? "

" Because I wished to divert suspicion from myself, and I owed Miss Mervyn a grudge ; and Mrs Ray, who was sweet on Mr Charteris then, promised me a large reward if I got her so suspected that she would be obliged to leave the place."

" Did Mrs Ray know that this was not Mr Charteris ? "

" I cannot tell. She never said."

" Ask him where he got the ring which he said he drew off from the murdered man's finger," says the detective, looking up from his pocket-book.

"I went to the Priory to make all the inquiries respecting Mr Charteris's disappearance," says the man, when the question has been put. "Mrs Ray and I were talking together in his dressing-room, when my eyes fell on the signet-ring. I took it up quietly, and was putting it on and off my finger while she was talking. She never seemed to notice it. After a while I laid it down ; but when her back was turned I put it into my pocket."

"As neat a bit of villany as ever I pieced together!" exclaims Mr Dowling, looking grimly at the unconscious man. "Oh, what a thing it is to have a chap sleeping before you as sweetly as a babe, and doing his very best to commit himself all the time ! What a sight of trouble we should be saved, if we could get a few more treated in the same way ! "

"Have you written all down ? " asks Mr Herrick, sternly.

"Yes, sir."

" Then I think there is no need to ask anything more," says the old lawyer.

" Shall I wake him now ? " demands the
mesmerist.

" Yes—no ; stay ! Bid him remove his
disguise first."

The sleeper obeys. He wrests off the close-
fitting wig and the grey eyebrows, and stands
revealed before his accusers, the smooth, sleek
Inspector Budd. Yet he is not quite the
same as of yore, for his face is haggard and
thin, his eyes are sunken and lustreless, the
brow is scored with many a deep furrow,
and the close-cropped hair, over which the
disguising covering fitted so admirably, is
streaked with patches of white.

" Now wake him ! " says Mr Herrick,
sternly.

There are a few slow waves of the strange,
mysterious hands, and then with a faint,
quivering sigh the eyes of the trapped and
guilty wretch unclose and rest upon the stern
accusing faces around him.

He springs to his feet. His face turns
grey and ashy, like the face of a corpse. Involuntarily his hands go up to his head and
he finds that his disguise is fathomed at last.
A low hoarse shriek passes his lips. He hurls
himself at the detective's sturdy figure, over-
turns him in his desperate strength and flies
to the door. It is barred and bolted! Howl-
ing like a caged wild animal, he turns back
and faces his persecutors.

"I think you had better make no resist-
ance," says the firm, cold voice of the
lawyer. "We are three to one, not counting Harris; and the house is surrounded by
police!"

"You have no warrant! You dare not
arrest me! What do you all mean?" shouts
the man, turning his glaring eyes from one
face to the other with the wild, ferocious terror
of an animal at bay.

"I accuse you of the murder of Gabriel
Lorton, a seaman, whose body was found in
Dead Man's Pool in the Beechhampton

Woods," says Mr Herrick, in a low, grave, relentless tone.

A shudder shakes the figure of the guilty, cowardly wretch. His eyes turn wildly, appealingly from one face to the other.

" I never did it ! " he says. " What proof have you ? "

" The best proof possible," answers Mr Herrick, sternly. " Your own confession while you slept. Nevertheless, you shall have a fair trial ; by that you must abide."

The ghastly incredulous stare which met this charge, fades and changes into one of abject fear. Without a word or plea, without an expression of doubt, the man drops upon his knees, grovelling in abject, miserable terror at the feet of his accuser, rending the air with shrill quavering cries for pity and for mercy.

" Seek them where your victim and accuser stands," is the old lawyer's relentless response. " Man will but deal back to you the mercy you showed to him ! "

CHAPTER IX.

THE snow is covering all the quaint
old gables of Mervyn Court and
spreading a spotless, dazzling car-
pet over the walks, lawn, and garden-beds,
when Yolande once more comes home.

White, pale, and fragile as any snowdrop
she looks herself, but for all that she declares
she is perfectly well and strong, though a little
anxious still for that milder air of the south
which is to work such wonders in her health.
The old master of the Court rouses himself
to some dim perception of his beloved child's
presence. She always hovers about him, sings
to him, talks to him, ministers to him as no
one else can do, her dearest reward being
some brighter gleam in the fading eyes, some

stronger pressure of the frail old hand, that once could give so true and hearty a grip to friends long since forgotten by his fading memory.

It brings the tears to Yolande's eyes to receive the tender greetings which are lavished upon her—to see Arthur's face grow brighter and his boyish eyes fill with tears of joy, and Miss Skipton's chocolate visage beam with welcome, while all the old servants crowd round her with loving words and greetings; and later on old Doctor Deane and his wife and the Hargraves come in, and there is pleasant talk and discussion, and no one says a word that might awaken painful memories. The pale, lonely girl moves among them all, with her wistful eyes and low, sweet voice, thinking, with strange subdued pain, of the lover who is to her as the dead, and missing in all the crowd of loving faces, that one face far tenderer and more loving still.

Though his name is never breathed by her lips, it is ever in her heart, lying there as

the dead lie in our memories; for to her it
must be indeed as if he were dead henceforth;
to think of him living is to destroy the hard-
won composure that, though it deceives others,
can never even for one brief, blessed moment
deceive herself.

.   .   .   .   .   .

Yolande is only to be at home a week, just
long enough to make all the necessary pre-
parations for that long stay in the south,
whither they are all bound, except Arthur.

During all that week she never leaves the
precincts of the Court. She knows that the
Charteris family are at the Priory. She has
heard various rumours of the accident, which
was so nearly fatal to both, but she has
not trusted herself to ask for particulars.
Sometimes she thinks that moment of mutual
danger may have softened Denzil's heart. At
all events, he and his wife are together now,
and so his thoughts of her must be kinder
than they were.

Is there not exquisite pain in that idea for

the brave girl who urged him to that distasteful duty ? Ah, well she knows it—too well, when the sharpness of agony pierces her at the thought of her rival's loveliness, subduing and softening the rancour of her husband's feelings, winning back some warmth to the chilled and desolate heart that once was vowed to her who mourns him now !

" In time he will forget," she tells herself again and again. " Oh, Heaven, that I might learn the lesson too ! "

When Sunday morning comes round Yolande does not go to church with the others ; she cannot bring herself to sit in the old accustomed place, and see perchance in the well-known Beechhampton pew the faces of Denzil Charteris and his wife ; so she lets the others depart, and walks up and down the warm conservatories with her father for his usual morning exercise, and then leaves him settled for his nap in his great deep arm-chair, and, wrapping herself in her warm furred cloak, she goes out.

It is a crisp, cold morning. The ground is frozen hard under foot, the trees are hung and garlanded with icicles, and the sky overhead is of a clear steel-like blue. The fresh air and brisk exercise bring the old-rose tint back to Yolande's pale cheeks, and send the blood tingling and coursing through her veins. She leaves the Court by the old lodge-gate and turns to the road that leads to the woods she used to love so well.

How quiet and still everything is! Not a human being is visible anywhere. A robin chirps on a tree near by, a ray of sunshine falls through the white glittering boughs, and its dazzling lustre is caught and reflected by the shining crystals on every side.

She leans against the well-remembered stile leading to the short cut to Beechhampton— the stile on which she and Arthur, and Vi and Enid, cut their initials in the old childish days that seem so long gone by. She leans there, and through the frosty air comes the clear, sweet chime of bells. The girl leans her head on her hands, and a sudden rush of tears comes to the hidden eyes. It is only in solitary moments like this that she gives way to such weakness ; but it is a hard task to forget, and, to such a nature as Yolande's, impossible. The bells cease at last ; the robin flies to chirp his little song at some cottage lattice ; and the girl, leaning so wearily against the stile, raises her eyes, with deep dark circles round them, and her face full of an unutterable anguish, and looks straight into the face of the man from whom she parted in such bitter agony a few brief weeks before.

She recoils a step. He is on one side of the stile, she on the other—divided by a barrier so slight, yet strong as that invisible barrier which keeps them apart now—with no kiss or hand-touch given or asked.

Denzil speaks first.

" How ill you look ! " he says. " Yolande, is it true you are going away ? "

" Yes," she answers, with a quietness that surprises herself. " We leave to-morrow."

" I—I hope it will do you good," he says, with a dangerous tremor in his voice. " I did not think you were so changed! "

He stands gazing at every line and feature of the lovely little face, so unutterably pathetic now in its mute brave sorrow, with the childish quivering lips, the dark and sorrowful eyes drooping before his own too eager gaze. Her name passes his lips—he makes no effort to restrain himself—in a second he has leaped the barrier that keeps them apart, and stands beside her, folding his arms round the little trembling figure, half mad with the rapture and the longing that seize him as he feels her heart beats answering his own, as he sees the warm, rich colour flushing over cheek and brow beneath his passionate words.

" If I could only bear your sorrow, or lighten it ! Oh, my love—my love ! "

She is too weak, too startled to resist him. Passive as a child, she rests in the strong clasp of those arms that were to have made the shelter and refuge of her life once—that now— She shudders at the thought, and strives to release herself.

"Oh, Denzil," she moans, "you only make it harder—thus! Do you forget—"

"Forget?" he says, bitterly. "Is it so easy? While the blood of life runs through my veins, while my heart beats at the mere delight of your presence, the mere sound of your name, I shall never forget!"

"I did not mean that!" she says, piteously. "I suppose it is wicked and wrong of me not to wish to lose your love; but I meant, do you forget—her? We have no right to stand thus, now! The more difficult the task we have to learn, the more we should avoid all temptation to forget it. Denzil, it is well we have to part. I do not think I could bear to be here and see you and her—together!"

"You would not see that," he answers, coldly, releasing her from his embrace now, and stepping back a pace or two as he speaks. "Have you not heard?"

"Heard what?"

" Of the accident that so nearly killed us both. Oh, Yolande, if it only had ! It has crippled her for life. She never moves off the couch ; the doctor says she never will ! "

" Oh, how sad ! " cries the girl, turning very pale.

" I wonder you do not say it is a judgment upon her. Many women in your place would."

" Oh, no ! " she says, shuddering. " I am not so wicked, so unforgiving ! Deeply enough she has wronged us both, Denzil. Yet I know that, with all her schemes and all her beauty, she has not been able to win what she would have given all else to obtain —your love ! "

" You are right ! " he answers, with the old passionate gleam in his dark eyes. " My little darling, no one in all the world can ever win that from you."

She looks up at him, and both are silent— a long, dangerous silence, sweet, soft, and full of exquisite memories, but doomed to an awakening of tenfold bitterness. As, after some bright dream, when the loved and lost return, we awake to the double misery of loss and grief, so they too awake to the memory of the present, the knowledge of the parting that lies before them.

"You need never fear that," he goes on, softly. "Such love is not to be taken or given at will. But, oh, Yolande, what right have I to burden your life with a faithfulness I may never be able to repay? I ought not to be so selfish. If you in time to come, think it possible to find happiness in new ties with any other, and thus forget the fatal error which has darkened both our lives, believe me, I will never reproach you! I cannot say I shall not suffer; for a man of my years, who loves as I love you, cannot easily un-loose the memories which bind him, or tear his idol from his heart, without desperate suffering. But you must not think of me, if—such a time ever comes!"

His voice grows almost inaudible in its anguish, bravely as he strives to steady it.

She looks up into his face with a strange smile on her own—such a smile as a martyr at the stake might wear, as a woman only gives in her agony who would fain comfort at any cost one she loves.

" Oh, hush, Denzil ! Do you still mean to give me the old character ? Would you have me believe it possible to break vows I deem as sacred as a marriage oath ? Love or happiness with any other is utterly impossible ! It sounds an insult to speak of it ! I should not be worthy of that love I hardly dared hope to win, could I give to another what was sealed and sacred to you."

He bends his head to conceal his agitation. He can find no words to answer her now.

" How noble you are ! " he murmurs at last. " To think what I have lost, to think how I wronged you ! Oh, Heaven, the tortures of Tantalus are not more terrible than mine ! "

Seeing his anguish, her strength almost forsakes her. A heavy, hopeless sigh escapes her lips.

"I did not think I should meet you again," she says, sadly. "I thought you would be at church this morning, and I came out to say farewell to the old familiar landmarks. I shall not see them for so long, you know."

"And I did not even know you were home yet," he answers, raising his white haggard face ; doubly haggard and worn it looks in the sweet golden sunlight flooding earth and sky so lavishly. "I have been thoughtless too in keeping you standing here in the cold. You look so delicate still. Yolande"—and a sudden sharp anguish thrills his voice—" are you really better—stronger than you were ? "

"Do you mean, am I going to die, or go into a decline, or anything of that sort ? " she answers, with a bitter little laugh. " No, Denzil, it is only in novels girls do that sort of thing. I have got bodily strength to bring me through this, though I should not have believed it once ! "

"Don't speak like that," he entreats ; " I cannot bear it. Do you know, if anything

happened, it would seem to me as if I had
killed you—killed you by my own mad folly.
Oh, Yolande, how could I ever have believed
what I did ?   I have always been hasty and
given to forming passionate judgments—such
errors have marred my life before.   But surely
I must have been utterly insane to credit such
a tissue of lies as were told me !   You heard
about that girl at the school who stopped the
letters and sent the notice to the paper ? "

" Yes," answers Yolande ; " she always dis-
liked me.   But, oh, Denzil, don't talk about
that any more now !   Nothing can alter or
remedy it.   Regrets are so useless ! "

" True," he says, despairingly, as he walks
on beside her.   " Nothing can alter it.   My
jealous fury, which turned all faith in you to
utter disbelief, which rendered all the memories of your truth, your love, your vows,
of no avail, has indeed been punished ! "

" It must have been so hard," she returns,
never blaming him, never saying that a thou-
sandfold such testimony could not have de-

luded her into such utter madness as had led
him to forge the terrible fetters which bind
him now. " I do not wonder you doubted
me, Denzil. I suppose you thought I was
still playing the *rôle* of ' My Lady Coquette ' ? "

" Even that wrong I owe to her ! " he cries,
fiercely. " She sent you that odious valen-
tine, copying my handwriting as closely as
possible ! "

" How long ago it seems since I got that
unfortunate piece of paper," answers Yolande,
sadly, " and yet it will only be a year next
month ! "

" A year ! Oh, if it were only possible to
cut out this wretched, wasted year from my
life—to begin again with a new heart and
fresh hopes ! " he groans aloud. " Oh, my
darling, I cannot bear this ! Am I never to
see your face now ? Is all this cruel distance
to be between us, and no word or sign to
bridge it ? "

" Is it not best ? " she says, gently. " Ask
yourself, Denzil, whether we could do any

madder or more senseless thing than to meet even casually as we met to-day, knowing all that the past has told, that the future —forbids ? "

He turns deadly pale ; his whole frame quivers with an intensity of emotion that scarcely all the force of his strong will can curb or control.

"You are right indeed," he says. " I cannot see you and forget how wildly I love you. I cannot look on you and remember my own cold, unblessed life, in which you have no part or place now, and be calm as my honour demands, as your nobleness deserves. Heaven forgive me, I cannot ! And yet, oh, my darling, with all the width of oceans between us, should I not still sin in thought ? For, if love sanctifies a human tie in an absolute and unalienable fidelity, such love lives in my every memory of—you ! "

The low-breathed passionate words sweep like sweetest music over her aching, throbbing heart. She raises her eyes to his, heavy with unshed tears, eloquent with a love that equals his own in force, devotion, and strength.

"I do not envy her—now," she murmurs, tenderly. "For all she has robbed me of, how little has she gained! No, don't speak," she adds, hurriedly. "I should not say such words—perhaps they are wrong and unwomanly; but it seems to me that love cannot be given and recalled, even in view of a hundred marriage rites; and yet, Denzil, as I said before, we must not meet again if we meet thus. It is but re-opening old wounds. You must see it too. Nothing will give us back our wrecked happiness, and, till we can meet calmly—as friends—we had better not meet at all. Now here we are close to the lodge gates. Say good-bye, Denzil, and let me go."

"Can I let you go?" he says, wildly, stretching out his arms once more to fold her to his aching, tortured heart.

She steps gently aside.

"No," she says, firmly, "I will not forget what is due to myself again, even if you forget what is due to—your wife."

"Are you so cold? Can you leave me thus?" he cries, passionately. "Heaven knows when we shall meet again! Am I to have nothing to remember of our last farewell?"

She looks at the wild, sad face, the imploring eyes, the white and trembling lips, and her strength almost breaks down.

"Listen," she says; and something in her voice calms the fiery tumult in his soul as by a spell. "I am not cold—I am not indifferent to your pain and misery. I will put the greatest trust in you that woman can put in man, for in telling you this I lay my life at your mercy. I will not rest in your arms; I will not suffer your kisses, because—oh, Denzil, why do you press me to say it?—if I did so, I should have no strength to bid you leave me again!" And, with bent head and cheeks shame-flushed, she moves swiftly away.

For a moment he stands there spell-bound.

" Oh, Heaven," he moans, " how she loves me ! What have I lost ? "

And to the hurrying figure, that turns not, nor looks back in the piteous shame, passion, and bewilderment that throb in every heart-beat, there comes across the white and silent road one low and bitter cry—the cry of a strong man in his agony and remorse. It finds an echo in her own despairing heart.

CHAPTER X.

N the softly-shaded boudoir which forms part of her suite of rooms lies the mistress of Beechhampton Towers.

The beautiful face is drawn by severe pain ; all its soft and delicate colouring has fled. That terrible accident, which was so nearly fatal, has left her a helpless cripple for life, dependent as a child on the attendance and ministry of others. Her plotting and scheming have done little for her, after all. She cannot enjoy even the outward semblance of all she has sacrificed her honour to win. The man she has wronged so deeply avoids all but the most ordinary intercourse with her. He pays her one visit in each day ; but his pity

for her sufferings is merely such as a stranger
might feel. Every comfort, luxury, and care
that money can command are hers ; but the
ministry of servants is at best a poor sub-
stitute for the devotion of love ; and, save
for her mother's languid sympathy, and his
stated visits, she is utterly desolate. Yet that
strange ill-fated love burns as deeply as ever.
Like a miser counting his gold, so does she
count those few blessed moments when her
husband's presence lightens her dreary solitude. She is racked with an aching longing
for the mere sound of his step, and the touch
of his hand. He gives her no other greeting,
nor has he given her such since the hour that
she won his empty heart in its reckless and
despairing rebound.

A terrible price indeed has she paid for her
bargain ! There are moments when, if she
were not so utterly helpless, she would put
an end to the existence that is one long,
maddening torture ; but all means to commit
this crime she once rashly attempted are

beyond her power now. She can only lie there suffering—suffering from day to day, yet finding even in bodily anguish no respite from the torments of her sin-stained soul.

It is Sunday evening. The bells are chiming soft and clear, the stars stud the heavens like myriads of glittering gems. The lamps in the boudoir are shaded, shedding a softened light over the exquisite room and the figure lying so still on the couch by the fire, with golden hair rippling over the white lace-edged pillows, and feverish restless eyes that gleam with unwonted brilliance as they turn from the clock on the chimney-piece to the door.

" You are sure Mr Charteris is in, nurse ? " she says, for the twentieth time.

" Quite sure, madam," answers the stately silk-robed matron beside her.

" I never knew him so late before," she murmurs, restlessly. " He always comes at six, and now it is nearly half-past. Nurse, send a message down to say I wish particularly to see him. I—I cannot wait any longer.

The woman rises and leaves the room. Five minutes more elapse and then she returns.

" Mr Charteris will be here immediately, madam," she says.

The beautiful marble-hued face glows with sudden rosy warmth, and the restless hands grow still.

" You can leave me now," she says. " I will ring when I want you." And with a stately curtsey the woman passes out.

Pauline lies back on her pillows, her eyes closed, her whole heart absorbed in that intense eager listening for the reluctant step that makes the sole music of her life. It comes at last ; strangely listless and reluctant it seems to-night ; and the face that bends over her in the usual conventional greeting bears a sorrow and an anguish on its haggard features greater even than usual.

" You sent for me," he says, coldly.

" Did you not mean to come ? " she asks.
" Had you forgotten ? "

" I suppose I had," he answers, wearily, as
he sinks into the chair beside her couch.
" How are you to-day ? "

" Why do you ask that ? " she cries, fiercely.
" You know that each day, each hour, you
wish me dead! Why do you feign this interest in my health or welfare ? "

He is silent. His eyes turn to the fire
and rest there.

" If you only sent for me to utter these old
reproaches, I had better leave you again ! " he
says, sternly, at last.

" Oh, no—oh, no ! " she half sobs, stretching out one white fragile hand to stay him.
" How cruel, how hard you are ! Do you not
know that in all the long, torturing hours of
day and night I have only one thing to
look forward to—your brief visit ? Will you
shorten even that ? "

" I have no wish to add to your pain or
sufferings," he says, more gently ; " but for

Heaven's sake spare me needless taunts! I have enough to suffer without them!"

She looks at him with a fierce and passionate scrutiny. Her hand tightens its hold on his arm.

"You have seen—her!" she says.

The blood rushes to his face. He shrinks away as if from the insult of a blow.

"Well?" he says, with that cold hauteur which has made friends and enemies alike think twice before provoking Denzil Charteris.

"Oh, Heaven!" she moans, dropping her face on her hands and quivering with a passion of jealous rage and baffled love. "And here I lie like a log, a half-dead inanimate block, while you and she make love as though you had no wife!"

"Pauline," he says, with a sternness that awes her even in that outburst of wild, unrestrained passion, "if you wish for even the hollow semblance of peace between us, never desecrate her name by uttering it to me! Wrongs like mine are not easy to forget. Do not rouse the madness in my nature again. You call yourself my wife. Be sure that so much honour is still mine as to make me respect that title. Though you lie on that couch for twenty years you need fear no rival, but you have never had my heart, and therefore you cannot complain of losing its possession."

"How cruel you are," she sobs—"how cruel! Was I not fair as she? Was my love not a thousand times stronger? Had I not your love first, before even her shadow crossed your path? Can I win nothing from you—not even a kiss, a touch, a tender word, to lighten my weary journey to the grave?"

How pale and pleading and lovely she looks in her helplessness! The tears stream down her cheeks, the great billowy masses of hair float over her couch, her arms are stretched towards him in passionate despair; and yet, intensely as he pities her, her words only open his wounds afresh, her face only grows dark and abhorrent in his sight at the remembrance of the treachery that dims its beauty.

"I pity you," he says, with that cold gentleness which hurts her more than any anger. "But you know what you ask is impossible!"

She looks up at his averted face, and her own grows grey and colourless with the anguish of a great despair.

"How did she make you love her so?" she wails. "You used not to be so passive or cold; and I, who would lay my life down to win one tender word, can gain nothing from you but abhorrence. Is it because I sinned?"

"Because you sinned?" he echoes, bitterly. "That word is too light for your deadly, treacherous wrong. Had you sinned in a moment of anger, a fit of jealousy, the desperation of frenzy, I might have judged you less hardly; but you worked and planned with the cunning and deliberateness of a revengeful, merciless woman. You spared no pains, you brought the basest tools— Faugh! It sickens me to think a woman could be so utterly vile!"

"I own it now!" she cries, shrinking beneath the piercing scorn of his words. "Will you never forgive me—never?"

"I am no hypocrite," he says, bitterly. "If I could forgive you I might be a happier man; but my wrongs are too new and fresh —I cannot!"

"No; because you love that little coquette; because she has come here to win you from your duty to a dying wife—because—oh, because I have done you a greater wrong in living than any that has gone before!" she cries, with the old wild ungovernable passion in her face and voice.

He rises from his seat.

"Further discussion is useless," he says quietly. "Such violent agitation must be injurious to your health. I will call your attendant."

"No, no! For pity's sake stay a moment longer, Denzil!" entreats the wretched woman. "I cannot let you leave me thus. I repent of my wrong-doing—I acknowledge it now.

And, oh, husband, if I sinned it was because I loved you ! Oh, be merciful in this my hour of punishment ! Say you forgive me ! Oh, Denzil, in pity say it ! Your anger kills me !"

He pauses, and looks with white set face and sad stern eyes upon the wreck that suffering and passion have made of this once most beautiful, brilliant woman. She has touched a dangerous chord while praying for that forgiveness ; but he knows that his wrongs are indeed avenged by a Hand mightier and juster than that of man.

He walks over to the window, the throbbing of his heart nearly stifling him, the anguish of that struggle within his breast blinding his eyes to the calm and peaceful beauty of the night on which he gazes.

Panting and exhausted his wife falls back on her pillows, the moisture of weakness on her brow, the pallor of deadly faintness on cheek and lip.

The moments pass. The man looking out with sad and agonized eyes on the peaceful loveliness of the scene is wrestling with the strongest and fiercest temptation his life has yet known. He thinks of his cruel wrongs, of his darling's pale, changed loveliness, of the gloomy future stretching before them both—of the days and nights filled with an exceeding bitterness of regret that lie before him within the future. Then across the turmoil and tumult of his thoughts breaks the sweet music of the distant bells. A great peace that is in itself relief steals over his aching heart. He bows his head on his hands. The sob that bursts upward from his heart is half a prayer.

" Oh, Heaven, give me strength ! "

A few moments later he turns back and approaches the couch. The lovely anguished eyes look up in frantic terror to his own. He bends over the prostrate figure and lays his hand upon the head where shame has placed its unsightly crown, and honour's golden circlet has for ever been displaced.

" Pauline," he says, in low soft tones, " Heaven knows I never thought to speak

such words to you as you have prayed me
to speak. But I have no right to set myself
up as a judge of others. My own life has
not been so guiltless or so pure that I should
condemn you for falling under the force of
such tempting as beset you. All loftier,
nobler, purer hopes, are forbidden in such a
strange union as ours ; but at least there shall
be peace. I will do my best to think as
gently of you as I can, to smooth the rough,
hard path by which you are to travel. I
cannot say I forgive you all at once—my
heart is too sore still—but I will strive to
forget your wrong-doing, and I will not reproach you with it again."

For a moment she gazes at him in wondering, incredulous joy ; then she catches his
hands in both her own and bears them to
her lips, while the flood-gates of penitence
are opened, and her tears flow forth in purer
streams than have ever left those haughty
eyes since childhood. When she grows
calmer, she looks up at her husband's pitying

face—remorse, regret, and misery still shadow-
ing her own.

" You are nobler than I thought, Denzil,"
she whispers, faintly. " Bend down—close—
closer. I am spent and exhausted now, but
I will give you your reward."

He stoops towards her in faint wonder, and
a whisper, wrung from the very depths of
her sinful, passionate nature, reaches his ear.

" I wanted your forgiveness — freely. I
would not win it by a bribe. But I heard
to-day—that in—six months more—you will
be—free ! "

As the last word leaves her lips, strength
forsakes her. Through all her misery she
has never suffered as she suffers now, when
she knows that her sin has availed her
nothing, that an inexorable fate will ere
long part her from the man she has risked
honour, happiness, life, and truth to win.
She sinks back on the pillows in a long and
death-like swoon, while the effort of that
fiery struggle leaves him too sad and heart-

wrung for even the new-born hope she has whispered to stir one blissful thought of future happiness within his breast.

.   .   .   .   .   .

"If you please, sir, Mr Herrick is in the library, and wishes to see you on special business."

Denzil Charteris gives a glance at the sleeping woman, lying wrapped now in the deep dreamless slumber of exhaustion, and softly leaves the room. Strangely weary and worn does he feel and look as he descends the stairs and enters the room where the old lawyer waits—so worn and so altered that Mr Herrick's first words are,—

"Good Heaven, Charteris, your accident must have been more severe than we imagined! You look as if you had just recovered from a long illness!"

"Yes ; I have suffered a good deal," answers Denzil, mechanically. "But pray sit down. I suppose you have come about the old business ? "

"Yes," says the lawyer quietly; "I have come to tell you we shall settle the affair without troubling you at all."

"How?"—and the pale haggard face lights up with momentary interest.

"We have caught the fellow, and he has confessed," answers Mr Herrick; "so there is no need now to call upon you for that document. I am glad of it. Private family matters would have been sure to be raked up, and that wouldn't have been pleasant."

"But how is it? Who has caught him?" asks Denzil in surprise.

"An uncommonly clever fellow I got from Scotland Yard. He was up to the queerest dodge I ever heard of. I'll tell it to you in as few words as I can."

And forthwith he relates to the quiet listener the whole of that eventful plot by which Budd was discovered.

"It would read queerly enough in a book," says the lawyer; "but seeing is believing; and, though I was much against the experiment at

first, I must say I never saw anything more
successful. Even now," he adds, looking
round with a grave, reluctant glance, " I seem
to hear that cry of fear and baffled rage with
which he awoke, knowing he was trapped,
despite all his caution. He was nearly
through our hands too, for we found out
afterwards that the next day he was going to
Liverpool in a new disguise, and I suppose
from there he would have sailed to America or
California ; and a precious job we should have
had to catch him again. However he's safe in
Colston gaol now, and will be tried at the
next assizes."

" No wonder they could not identify the
body if such a long time had passed since the
murder was committed ! " exclaims Denzil
Charteris, interest in the strange narrative
replacing for a time the indifference he has
hitherto felt.

" No ; and it was just like that parcel of
boobies to be led by the nose in the first instance, and declare the body was yours because

Budd said it was yours. What a fool he was though ! He must have known that sooner or later you would return, and so it was useless to make out you were dead ! "

" Perhaps he counted on the length of time I might be absent. I had cause enough then to hate the place, Heaven knows ! " exclaims Charteris. " That fellow was a mean spy always ; perhaps he knew the reasons that made me leave so abruptly."

" Well, there is no need for you to do anything now but settle down quietly here with your wife and—forgive me, Charteris," adds the lawyer, breaking off abruptly. " How could I have been so foolish as to forget what has happened ? Do the doctors give no hope ? "

" No."

It is a strangely cold unloving response for a newly-wedded husband ; but the old lawyer knows better than to suppose a man like Denzil Charteris would bare his heart to the pity of any human creature.

For a moment they are both silent : then Mr Herrick rises and says,—

"I should not have intruded on you, Charteris, on such a day, and at a time when your heart must be indeed heavy with anxiety, had it not been that I felt my news might be some relief. But I will not detain you longer ; only be sure that I feel and sympathise with you now !"

"'Thank you," answers Denzil, curtly ; "you are very kind. But no sympathy can ease my burden ; I must bear it alone !"

The old man wrings his hand, with a glance of deep commiseration at the worn and melancholy face, so strangely, sadly changed ; and then, without further words, he leaves him.

"How he must love her !" he thinks as he leaves the house. "And yet he told me once he would never marry her !"

.   .   .   .   .   .

For long hours on that quiet Sabbath night did the master of Beechhampton sit there in his library, never stirring nor moving, his head bowed on his folded arms, a tempest of passionate and stormy feelings raging within his heart.

None but himself ever knew what an almost superhuman effort it had required to speak those words to the woman whose hand had twice dealt out to him the bitterest suffering of his life. Every time he entered her presence and saw her in those rooms he had in fancy prepared and beautified for his lost love, his heart was stabbed with a fierce, sharp regret. At every tone of her voice and every glance he felt afresh the bitter sting of that most base betrayal; he felt inclined to curse that moment of insane tempestuous fury when her words had goaded him to a course from which there was no possible return. He knew that if she had been as she was but a few weeks before, he could never have forgiven her; and even now, though she lay on a bed of suffering, from which death alone could release her, it

seemed to him but a just retribution for her
treachery to his innocent love. For himself
he would not have cared ; but that look to-
day on the changed sweet face that had been
so radiant and so fair—that strange shadowy
dread, which had haunted him ever since he
looked his passionate farewell at the slight
fragile figure — these recurred again and
again, to torture him with a ˙fear beyond
all he had ever known. These brought
him to his knees, bowed his proud head,
and taught his stubborn heart such prayers
as it could only have learnt in the fire of
suffering.

In that terrible struggle between wrath
and pity, between the memory of wrongs
done to him, and compassion for the poor
broken wreck of womanhood who prayed
his forgiveness for those wrongs, he had
striven, with the first purely unselfish force
his moral nature had ever known, to forget
what she had done, to remember only what she
suffered. Hatred and resentment faded slowly

away. He knew he had no right to condemn
when he too was so far from faultless; and
he was glad he had granted her prayer ere
he knew that Death would so soon be his
avenger.

Slowly and solemnly to-night there passed
before him in stran ge review the events and
incidents of his own life, the errors that pride
had led him into with the recklessness of an
uncontrollable will, the hasty doubts and
passionate judgment that had marred his
prospects of happiness and had left him
helpless in the hands of a designing
woman.

He remembered how one betrayal in his
early youth had hardened him to all belief
in the purity and single-heartedness of woman,
how with reckless and vehement passion he
had loved, and with equal recklessness and
vehemence had turned to utter disbelief in
the object and worthiness of that love. A
thousand memories of childhood, youth, and
manhood haunted him to-night. He gave no

heed to time as the hours rolled on. His
solitude was undisturbed. All external sur-
roundings were forgotten, and in that long and
terrible vigil perhaps a spirit of good wrestled
with his own, as in the days of the old world
that Heaven-sent messenger wrestled with
the patriarch, yet, after the struggle and the
pain, left a blessing behind.

.   .   .   .   .   .

Ere the party from Mervyn Court start the
next morning, a tiny note is put into Yolande's hand. It bears no signature, it
addresses her by no name ; but she knows
only too well whose hand has penned the
brief hopeful lines.

"Take every care of yourself," it says.
" Remember, your health is infinitely too
precious to be trifled with. Above all, keep
up a brave heart, and hope for the best.
Something tells me that happiness may yet
be ours. When night is darkest dawn is
nearest. Heaven for ever keep and bless

you, and guard you with safer care than
mortal love can do ! "

And, with that letter resting ou her heart,
Yolande sets out on her journey, feeling
strangely comforted.

CHAPTER XI.

IN the sweet rich air of southern lands,
with their blue skies and fresh winds,
cool with a tempered coolness that
rarely visits northern winters, Yolande grows
stronger and more like her old bright self.

The party stay for two months at Nice,
and then wander on lazily and carelessly from
place to place, avoiding tourists' haunts and
generally choosing the quietest and most unknown villages for their resting-place. Tra-
velling across Tuscany, they halt one evening
at Montepulto, that exquisitely-situated little
spot, with its scattered high-roofed houses,
its groves of chestnuts, its pale-grey groves
of olives, its many vineyards and thickets of
genista and myrtle and acanthus.

" How beautiful ! " cries Yolande. " What is the name of the place, Castrona ? " she asks the courier.

" Montepulto, signora," he answers, and forthwith launches into a description of its vineyards and olive-groves and vines, to which none of the party pays the slightest attention.

" We will stop here," cries Yolande, eagerly. " Is there an inn ? "

The courier answers in the affirmative ; and shortly afterwards they dismount from the rickety conveyance which has brought them from their last halting-place, and dazzle and bewilder the landlord of the shabby little inn by their number, the beauty of the girls, and the many wants of the whole party, as explained by the courier.

It turns out that there is another Englishman here too, a tourist ; and the landlord, with many apologies, hopes the illustrious *Inglese* will not object to his presence, as there is but one public room. Enid horrifies

Miss Skipton by declaring that the stranger's presence will make it all the jollier. Then the three girls rush off to look at their bedrooms. Enid and Yolande must share one, Miss Skipton and Vi the other; that matter is soon settled. Then Yolande comes down again to look after her father and see that he is comfortable. The old man is not half so feeble as he used to be, though his memory is still a blank, and his talk placid and simple as a child's.

" I think I will go out and look about me for little while," she says, after these matters have been satisfactorily arranged.

" Don't get lost!" cries Miss Skipton, anxiously.

" And don't fall in with our fellow-traveller. I mean to be the first to discover him," adds Enid.

And, with a laughing assurance that she will avoid both contingencies if possible, Yolande leaves the inn and saunters forth.

It is a lovely day ; already the breath of

spring seems in the air, and the young grasses gleam like a pale green sea as they spread over the brown earth once more. The young leaves wave, the young birds sing, the throbbing, pulsing, quivering beat of life is everywhere ; and the girl moving amidst it all feels to the very core and centre of her being the joy of its loveliness, the passion of its memories. No one guesses aught of the burden she carries in her heart, so bravely and uncomplainingly is that burden borne ; but her thoughts are rarely absent from that one place where her lover lives and waits, and struggles along that stony path of duty, which she has bidden him follow.

Not one whit less does she love him than she did, but that love is known only to herself and Heaven. She asks no pity or sympathy from any living being. Who could understand her, or judge him as she can judge him, or think of him so tenderly that there is no room in all the loving, trusting heart for any thought of wrong to enter ?

With musing eyes downbent, with thoughts absorbing heart and mind to utter forgetfulness of time and place, she moves along, a fair living picture in that fair scene. Sorrow does not kill, nor suffering either ; and, though both have left their traces on the once-brilliant beauty of the girl, she is not one whit less fair than she was.

Her absorbed reverie is disturbed at last. Along the narrow path she treads another footstep echoes. She raises her eyes, and sees approaching the figure of a man, young, stalwart, clothed in a light-grey travelling-suit, his head bent—as hers had been but a moment before—his stick scattering the pebbles at his feet, or switching off, in utter absence of mind, the young heads of the shining grasses.

" It is the fellow-traveller, I suppose," thinks Yolande, with a slight feeling of annoyance.

In an instant the approaching figure pauses, looks up, and then, with a cry of bewilderment rather than of pleasure, Yolande sees before her the well-remembered face of Lance Stapleton.

"Lance!" she cries, eagerly, and her hand is outstretched in greeting; and the wonder and surprise of seeing him bring the rosy colour to her face in flattering warmth and brilliance.

"Why, Lance, how did you come here? Have you dropped from the clouds? How glad I am to see you!"

He makes no response to her enthusiastic welcome. He only stands looking silently at her face, a great pain gnawing at his heart, a great sorrow darkening his eyes.

"Are you not glad to see me?" she says, disappointedly. "You have not spoken a single word."

"I—I was so surprised," he stammers, feebly.

"Yes, I daresay you were," she says, laughing a little at the remembrance of his astonished face. "And so will the others be when they see you. I suppose you are the

English gentleman staying at our inn, whose company is to be inflicted upon us? We are all here, you know—papa and the girls and Miss Skipton. We shall be quite a family party again."

He is still silent. His eyes never leave her face.

" Have you been ill ? " he asks.

" Yes," she answers, flushing nervously. " But I am all right again now—quite strong and well, Lance, I assure you."

" You don't look it."

" Never mind my looks," she says, impatiently. " Tell me how you came here, and if you are going to stop."

" I don't know," he answers, absently. " I —my plans are very unsettled. I—I suppose your husband is here too ? "

" My husband ? "

The girl recoils as though he had struck her, and every drop of blood recedes from her face, leaving it white as death.

" Oh, Lance," she cries, clasping her hands

and turning her sorrowful eyes away from his startled face, " is it possible you have not heard ? "

" Heard what ? "

" That Denzil Charteris is married ? " she says, with a quietness that amazes herself.

" Married ! and not to you, Yolande ? Are you dreaming ? "

" Oh, I wish I were, I wish I were ! " she cries piteously, all her self-command swept away by the sympathy and tenderness in his gaze and voice.

" It seems all so strange," Lance continues, moving on beside her through the pale green olive woods. " When I saw him last he was so full of joy and happiness, I guessed his secret without a word. He said he would bring you home as soon as ever it was pos-sible. What has come between you ? Has he played you false, or have you—"

" No," she interrupts. " Treachery parted us—a woman's treachery. She is now his wife. I cannot tell you all the wretched story, Lance ; it is too painful still. You must ask Enid ; she knows."

" I do not want to ask any one what you withhold from me," he says, slowly. " It is enough that you are parted. There is no need to ask if you are faithful still, Yolande ; I can see it in your face."

" Faithful ! " she repeats, with momentary forgetfulness of the pain she deals her old. lover. " I shall always be that, Lance. The cant of society calls it a sin, I suppose, when a girl refuses to forsake and forget the man to whom her heart is given because between them lies the barrier of impossibility ; but to me it seems no crime to be true, as I vowed and promised to be true, simply because he cannot marry me. I gave him my heart. Can I recall it because treachery has drawn him from my side ? No. I shall never marry now ; but, all the same, I have no blame for him. Wrong has been stronger than right, as it often is ; but, when I think of all he suffers, I have only pity, no blame. It is so much worse for him than for me."

" I—I wish I could understand," says Lance, pale and bewildered. " Who has come between you, Yolande."

" Pauline Ray," she answers, her voice very low and soft.

" His cousin ? And they are wedded, you say ? " Lance murmurs.

" Yes," she says, simply. " And I am that most deplorable of beings, Lance, a girl who loves a married man ! "

" Don't, Yolande ! " he cries, the bitterness of her voice stabbing his faithful heart with sharpest pain. " You don't know what you are saying. It is horrible to hear you speak like that ! "

" It sounds wicked, I suppose," she says, with forced calmness. " I have no doubt a proper-minded young person would have immediately returned his letters, given back his ring, and—forgotten him. Well, I am not a proper-minded young person, for I have done none of these things. I have only avoided him for his own sake, even more than for mine."

It seems strange to her that she can speak so much more easily and frankly to Lance than to anyone else who knows her sad story ; but she does. And he sees now, even as he saw in the old by-gone days, how utterly hopeless his own ill-fated love must be. Bound or free, it is all one. She has given her love once ; she will never give it again. Her faith, sorely as it has been tried, is still unshaken. But he feels a shudder of horror through all his strong young frame as he hears her reckless words, as he sees that her lost lover is her lover still, that she does not for one moment seem to think of him as another woman's husband.

Yet what can he say ? She is not a conventional girl ; she is not a well-drilled society machine, acting, thinking, and expressing herself after the most approved and correct pattern. Hers is a heart that can sweep all paltry considerations away, and look danger calmly in the face. A love that is unlawful might make some women weak as water; it only strengthens her amidst the fiery suffering it brings.

Had Lance Stapleton known all the facts of the case, he might not have blamed her, even in thought ; but he knows nothing save that Denzil Charteris is the husband of his beautiful intriguing cousin, and that Yolande loves him no whit the less for that fact.

" I know you are wondering at me, Lance," she says, presently. "I daresay you think I am very wicked to speak like this ; but indeed I cannot help it. Fidelity is a rare-enough virtue, and when it exists seems always to exist in the wrong place. To me it is the very core and centre of love, keeping it true through evil report or good—through suffering, sin, or shame."

He looks in silent wonder at the beautiful face so eloquent with feeling, so pure and noble, that all thought of rebuke fades from his mind. He sees here a truth that is above all paltry considerations, that can be judged by no mere conventional rule, and his heart thrills with admiration, even though he knows such feelings are for ever vowed to his rival's cause.

" How we have all misunderstood you, Yolande ! " he says, with a deep sigh.

" Yes. I daresay you too thought I was only good for flirting· and waltzing and amusement," she says, with a faint smile. " It is so difficult to judge from the surface-view of character. I don't think I ever quite knew myself—what was really in me—till I learnt to suffer and endure."

" It is a hard lesson," he says, compassionately, looking with unspeakable sadness at the shadowed and pathetic beauty of the once bright, wilful face.

" Yes, but a necessary one. Perhaps it has done me more good than any one imagines. Life cannot be all sunshine—can it, Lance ? "

" Your life should have been," he cries,

passionately. " Oh, Yolande, what a treasure Charteris has thrown away ! Was he mad, that he did this thing ? "

She bends her head, a sudden flush of shame staining cheek and brow.

" I think he was," she says, hurriedly— " mad with grief and rage and distrust. They told him I was to be wedded to another ; it was even printed in the newspapers. Oh, Lance, you little know how cleverly that woman schemed to rob me of him, what arts she used to divide us both ! "

" But could he not trust you better ? Why did he hurry into the trap so readily ? Even if he knew you false, did that necessitate his marrying another woman ? "

" You do not know," she says, piteously, " you do not understand ! "

It hurts her unspeakably to hear her lover blamed by any other lips. She would have all judge him, as she in her tender love has done.

" No," he says, coldly, " you are right ; I do

not understand. Were I your brother I soon should."

She turns very pale, but her face grows cold with a haughty scorn that he has never seen it wear yet.

"Were you my—brother," she says, coldly and cuttingly, "you would have to learn what you must learn now—that I allow of no interference with matters that concern only me."

"But this does not concern only you," he rejoins, flushing angrily.

"If I choose to think so, it does. Oh, Lance," she cries dropping her cold tone suddenly and stretching out her hands in piteous appeal, "don't let us quarrel now! We have been friends so long, and I have enough to bear; don't you turn against me too!"

"Heaven forbid!" he says, with passionate fervour, taking the little trembling hands in both his own. "Deeply as your words wound me, Yolande, I cannot resent them. Let us try to forget what we have said."

"I don't want you to be cross with me," she remarks, a dangerous quiver in her voice as she meets his entreating eyes. "We were always good friends, you and I, Lance ; and I have not so many that I can afford to lose one."

"I will be your friend always," he answers, tenderly. "Even that cold tie is sweeter than the love of any other woman. Like yourself, Yolande, I own the virtue of fidelity."

She blushes deeply ; her eyes droop, her hands loose their clasp.

"I thought you had forgotten," she says.

"Forgotten!" he echoes. "Is it so easy, Yolande? Ask your own heart, and by its answer read mine."

She is silent. His words pain her deeply, because only too well does she know their meaning, only too well does she gauge their depths of pain. They move on together, neither of them speaking, each busy with sad and painful memories, each striving for outward calm despite that inward struggle.

CHAPTER XII.

OVING on with heedless feet and down-bent eyes, Yolande and Lance suddenly find themselves once more in the straggling village street; and there, standing at the inn-window, laughing and talking merrily together with the unrestraint and freedom of old acquaintanceship, Yolande sees her sister Enid and Sir Edward Llewellyn.

"A friend of yours?" questions Lance, seeing her start of surprise and the young baronet's bow of pleased welcome.

"Yes," she says. "We seem to be coming across all our old friends to-day. You are coming in surely?" she adds, as he pauses and extends his hand in farewell.

"Presently—not just now," he answers, hurriedly. "Excuse me, Yolande. I want a few moments to myself before facing strangers."

She makes no comment—only gives him her hand in farewell, and passes from his sight into the dusky archway of the inn.

"You here?" she cries, as a certain shame-faced, well-known countenance turns to her in gladdened welcome. "I really wonder whom we shall find next. One would think we had appointed Montepulto as a trysting-place for all our friends."

"I have only just arrived," he says, shaking hands warmly with her as he speaks.

"And were you not surprised to find us here?" asks Yolande.

"I—I cannot exactly say I was," he answers, in some slight confusion; "for, to tell you the truth, I followed you up from your last halting-place."

"Oh, indeed!" says Yolande. "And are you doing Italy also?"

" I—I think so," he answers, making a valiant effort to recover himself and look composed.

" Whom were you walking with, Yolande ? " interrupts Enid at this moment.

" Lance Stapleton. It turns out that he is our fellow-traveller who is staying here," she answers.

" Lance—dear old Lance here? Oh, how glad I am ! " cries Enid, with an enthusiasm that apparently does not awaken any sympathy on the part of Sir Edward.

" A friend of yours, Miss Enid ? " he asks.

" A most particular friend," Enid answers, emphatically. " We have known each other ever since we were children. He lives close to our place at home."

" Oh, indeed ! " he says, somewhat coldly.

" Do you know if we are going to have anything to eat, Miss Skipton ? " inquires Yolande, removing her hat and swinging it carelessly on one finger.

" I believe luncheon is coming up directly,"

answers the faithful *gouvernante.* "At least, Castrona said so a few moments ago."

"You will stay, will you not?" asks Yolande. "It will give us great pleasure; won't it, papa?"

"Yes, dear, yes," answers the old man, nodding placidly from his chair by the window.

"I should be most happy," says Sir Edward, rather stiffly; "but I fear I shall be spoiling your party."

"What nonsense!" exclaims Yolande. "We have got out of the way of ceremony here. We shouldn't ask you if we thought that."

"Is Lance coming soon?" asks Enid, mischievously.

"I believe so," answers her sister. "I will just run upstairs and leave my hat, and be down directly. Sir Edward, pray don't look so formal and punctilious! We are out of England now."

She runs away lightly, and the baronet turns to Enid, thinking how much prettier she has grown within these past few months, and how much more like Yolande.

" I suppose you admire Italy very much ? " he says, in a low voice, as though the remark was very confidential.

" Of course," she answers, demurely. " Its fine and equable climate, its radiant skies, its picturesque scenery, and its abundant and variegated floriculture render it indeed worthy of the enthusiasm poets and historians have lavished upon it."

" Why do you talk like that ? " he asks, half vexed, half laughing.

" I learnt it from the guide-book," she says, laughing too at his impatient tone. " I intend to say it always when I am asked that ridiculous question. I don't think my querists will pursue the subject for long, do you ? "

" No, I don't. Is that a hint to me ? "

" Well, it was so absurd," she answers, lifting her radiant lovely eyes to his. " Just as if I should only admire Italy, or like it !

Why, it takes one by storm! It makes
one want a new language to utter all one
feels!"

"Have you been to Florence yet?"

"No; but we are going. We shall make
a long stay there, I hope."

"Have you heard any news from home
since you left?"

"Nothing very particular. Arthur writes
from college; but he is of course full of
'longs' and 'shorts' and 'little go's' and
''varsity eights' and 'strokes' and training,
and goodness knows what all! His head is
running more on boat-racing than on books,
I should say!"

"But I mean from Ashbourne or Colston?"
says Sir Edward, gravely.

"No. We never look at a paper, and we
are so constantly moving about that our
letters never seem to find us."

"I have brought some news for your
sister," he says, dropping his voice so suspiciously that Miss Skipton eyes him with

duenna-like fierceness from her corner of the room.

"For Yolande? Oh, Sir Edward! Good or bad?" And the girlish laughing face grows strangely agitated as she puts the question.

"Good," he says, steadying his voice with an effort, but bravely speaking out what he has travelled all these weary miles to say. "Charteris's wife is dead!"

Enid is silent. It seems incredible for freedom to have come thus. Her heart almost stops beating, so agitated is she by the news.

"And is that why you are here?" she asks softly at last.

"Yes," he says, simply. "I thought I would not trust the news to post or printer. When shall I tell her?"

"Not here—not before us all!" cries Enid, hurriedly. "Wait till luncheon is over. I can scarcely believe it yet myself. You are sure it is true?"

"Sure. Do you think I should be here to deceive her?" he says, sternly.

"No, no—I know that!" she answers, with quick compunction. "But even newspapers lie sometimes. She is only just growing calm and reconciled to her fate."

"I trusted to no second-hand authority," he says. "I came direct from the Priory. I saw Charteris myself. I did not tell him I was coming here; but I think he knew."

"How good of you," she remarks, giving him a shy bewitching glance, "to take all that trouble for her!"

"Perhaps it was not all for—her," he says, with a look eloquent of meaning into the soft brown orbs. "I knew I should meet you again too."

"But that must have been a very secondary consideration," declares the little flirt, "because no one thinks anything of me when Yolande is by."

"I have thought of you very often," says the audacious young man, utterly ignoring Miss Skipton's Gorgon-like glances, "even when Yolande was by."

"Ah, there is Lance Stapleton passing the window!" cries Enid, jumping up with an effusive eagerness of welcome that secretly inspires her admirer with an intense desire to knock down the object of her interest, without further notice. "Oh, please excuse me, Sir Edward! I must go and see him!"

And Sir Edward bows and gnaws his moustache, muttering inwardly to himself,—

"D—n Lance Stapleton!"

CHAPTER XIII.

CRUSHED for a time by the bitter
knowledge of his hopeless love, Sir
Edward had yet risen from the
blow, manlier, braver, stronger. He was not
going to spend the rest of his days in pining
after what could never be his ; and he set
himself bravely and manfully to work to
conquer the passion that had been so sudden
and so sweet, that had ended in an awakening
so dark and desolate. His love had been like
some rich tropical flower blooming into vivid
summer life in the dull garden of his common-
place existence ; like a flower too it had been
short-lived, sweet, intoxicating. But he was
too wise to waste all that remained of his years
in lamenting its loss ; and he was surprised

himself to find how much easier the task
had become since Enid's face had smiled on
him. In days yet to come, when the old
wound is healed and the old smart no longer
stings with sharp pain at any touch or word,
he will turn for consolation to the bright
young comforter who has already done him
so much unconscious good, and she will make
his imperfect, half-spoiled life, a happy and
complete one.

At present, however, she is occupied in the
tantalising pursuit which seems inherent in
every woman's nature, of playing off one man
against another, lavishing all her words,
looks, and attentions on Lance Stapleton, to
the utter—apparent—exclusion of the unfortunate baronet. She piques him into con-
siderable wrath by this *ruse*, and then as
suddenly soothes him again by a soft glance,
a low whisper. Truly Enid is no unworthy dis-
ciple of her elder sister ; but she will never love
as faithfully as does " My Lady Coquette."

She—Yolande—is still unconscious of the

good news in store for her. In all her many portraits of her lost lover, she had never pictured Denzil as being free once more. He has either died, or she has drooped and faded beneath the long and weary struggle, a struggle all the fiercer and harder in that it is fought in secret, a struggle that would have gradually sapped her life-springs and given to the loving faithful heart but one dream of rest, one hope of peace—death! Yet Heaven has not so willed it. For once the hand of Fate is kind, and metes justice where justice is deserved. For once the long and faithful love that has been tried in the fire of suffering is destined to be rewarded ; and when, in the cool spring evening hour, she hears at last from Sir Edward's kind lips the sweet tidings of her lover's freedom, the shock of joy is almost more than her strength can bear.

The great heroic tenderness which has buoyed her up in the deep waters of trouble, fails utterly now in this moment of unlooked-for joy. White as death, she stands trembling in the

moonlight, listening to the words that are as
freedom to the captive, as reprieve to the
criminal, as the warm, fresh, delicious ecstasy
of liberty to the prisoner released from long
and almost hopeless captivity. Trembling like
a leaf in that moment of relief, she lifts up her
face to the man who has brought her such joy ;
and that one look of gratitude, that speechless
voiceless thanksgiving, quivering on her lips,
yet finding no utterance in mortal speech,
repays him for all the self-abnegation of his
task, and brings the tears to his own eyes in
kindred sympathy. Then, having told her all,
he leaves her to the solitude of a holier, sweeter
peace than ever her life has known in all its
days of sorrow, or of joy.

.   .   .   .   .   .

They are a merry, happy party enough now.
Enid is the life and soul of them all. Yolande
after the first prostration and exhaustion
brought on by the reaction of her unexpected
deliverance, grows sweeter, lovelier, more
fascinating than ever.

With the smile of spring over all the lovely lands through which they journey, life and love and peace come also to their hearts and lives. Even poor, sad, desolate Lance grows calmer and more comforted, though he knows in his lost love's eyes, lives the radiance of a hope that is to him as death, the light of joy rekindled from the ashes of a great and passionate sorrow.

.   .   .   .   .   .

Quite alone, and pale with watching and expectation, Yolande sits in one of the rooms in their pretty villa awaiting her lover's return.

Her head is bent on her hands; the light flickers down on her hair and turns it into richer gold. Her eyes are dark and wistful; for even this most exquisite moment is tempered by the shadow of the past.

Just so once before had she awaited his coming, and found in it her doom. A prayer is on her lips, a prayer of thankfulness for the great blessing that has been restored, a prayer for strength to bear it meekly, humbly, as one to whom a great and precious gift has been entrusted.

And while such thoughts are in her heart there comes through the hushed and fragrant silence, the sound of a footfall. She lifts her head—her colour comes and goes—her eyes grow bright and dark in the joy and fear of this expectancy. Then, with á rush of joy so keen that it is almost pain, she sees the face she scarce had thought to look upon again, save in dread and misery like that which had filled their last parting.

With one low glad cry of purest rapture she springs to meet him, feeling, as his arms close round her once again, as his lips rest on her own in passionate unspoken welcome, that neither life nor death can part her now from a love that will live through all time.

.   .   .   .   .   .

At the winter assizes the once esteemed and respected inspector finds the reward of long treachery and hidden guilt. From the moment he knew by what means his confession had been wrested from him he ceased to struggle. He even said it was a relief to find that it had all come out at last, for he had grown weary of concealment; and yet some instinct stronger than reason, more powerful than the longing for safety, had held him chained to that one spot which his crime had stained, which his sin had haunted.

.   .   .   .   .   .

Rose Bertram left school at Christmas, and soon after married a wealthy young Welsh landowner, who lived near Pwym Dyas and fell a victim to her large amount of personal charms and her pleasant, frank nature. Jane Croft was dismissed by Mrs Davies, at the request of Denzil Charteris, long before his wife's death, and took a situation as companion to an elderly dowager, who certainly avenges the sins of her youth upon her long-suffering victim. With all her cleverness,

Miss Croft has never succeeded in winning a husband, and has at last settled down into soured and discontented old-maidenhood.

Enid in two years' time consoled Sir Edward for his first misplaced affections, and made him very happy. Vi is still at the Court, and emulating her sisters' graces and witcheries as fast as she can. Yolande makes a lovely and gracious *chatelaine* at the Priory, and adores and is adored by her husband with a worshipping zeal that is the amazement of all their friends. Her father lives there with her, Arthur, Vi, and Miss Skipton reigning at the old Court.

The tragedy at Dead Man's Pool is long remembered and retailed by the chroniclers of Ashbourne ; but happily no other deed of violence has yet arisen to replace its interest. James Dowling—or rather John Clarke—received his reward and another handsome *douceur* from Denzil Charteris for the capture of Budd. That worthy hypocrite ended his career in the odour of sanctity, the chaplain at the gaol declaring he had never had a convict so creditable or so penitent.

THE END.

COLSTON AND SON, PRINTERS, EDINURGH.

www.ingramcontent.com/pod-product-compliance
Lightning Source LLC
Chambersburg PA
CBHW020604030726
47497CB00007B/2069